JANET AULISIO©1980

Look for these other TOR books by Fred Saberhagen

THE BERSERKER WARS
A CENTURY OF PROGRESS
COILS (with Roger Zelazny)
DOMINION
EARTH DESCENDED
THE FIRST BOOK OF SWORDS
THE SECOND BOOK OF SWORDS
THE THIRD BOOK OF SWORDS (Trade edition)

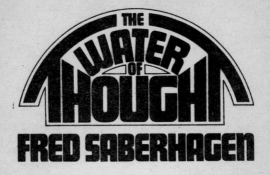

FRED SABERHAGEN

TOR

A TOM DOHERTY ASSOCIATES BOOK

THE WATER OF THOUGHT

Copyright © 1981 by Fred Saberhagen

A shorter version of this work was published © 1965.

First printing: May 1981
Second printing: April 1985

A TOR Book

Published by Tom Doherty Associates
8-10 West 36 Street
New York, N.Y. 10018

Cover art by David Mattingly

ISBN: 0-812-55290-3
CAN. ED.: 0-812-55291-1

Printed in the United States of America

Cover and interior illustrations

by Janet Aulisio

The Water of Thought

I.

In the dream a faceless figure came pacing after Boris. Clad in a groundsuit, it groped toward him with hands whose fingers writhed like snakes, menacing and venomous.

No, Boris told the figure, it's not me you want. Those are your hands, not mine. And then he realized that he was waking up.

He lay in the bottom of a little two-passenger sportboat with a float-cushion tucked under his head. The boat was pulled into the shore of a tiny river island, and the light of an alien though very Sol-like sun came dappling down on him through alien trees, making leaf-shadows of shapes that to Earth-descended eyes were subtly wrong. The sun reflected from the quiet water to shimmer upward on Brenda's laughing face and her dark brown hair as she bent over him.

Boris was blond and bony and tall, with innocent blue eyes in a rough face; it crossed his mind now that Brenda was his opposite in just about every physical detail. He had met her ten days ago, when he had arrived on the planet, and though he hadn't

JANET AULISIO ©1980

been alone with her for any length of time until today, he had been looking forward to the chance.

Her manner now was one of playful reproach and overlain with just a little concern. "I don't mind your dozing off," she told him. "But must you have nightmares?"

"I guess I must. Was I making noises?" He stretched luxuriously, trying to remember the dream. But already the burden of it was slipping away.

"What were you dreaming about?"

He sighed. The sound was part contentment with this, his waking world, part something else. "I think it probably had something to do with my last job."

Brenda became more sympathetic. His work impressed her. "Where was that?"

"Oh. Parsecs away from here."

"Well, of course. But what happened? If you don't mind my asking."

"I don't mind. What happened was a man on my crew opened his helmet when he shouldn't have. As simple as that. Something got in and began eating at him."

"Oh, horrible. Now I wish I hadn't asked. Was he . . . "

She had never heard of the man before, and still it hurt her personally to hear about it. "The medics saved him. He's getting a new face built."

Brenda looked at Boris silently for a long moment. Then with some hesitation she asked: "Did they blame you for it?"

"No." Boris sat up, making the boat rock soft ripples into the gentle river. He looked round at the peaceful green wilderness that filled island and shores alike. Hayashi was, or had been, a planeteer, not an infant. He shouldn't have needed extra warnings, and leading by the hand.

Once, more years and planets ago than he cared right now to think about, Boris had been young and green. Then a planeteering scheme of his had led to the drowning of a number of men. But why should he recall that old disaster now, on this pleasant afternoon? He didn't know. And why should Brenda immediately ask him if he had been blamed for what happened to Hayashi? Did he look guilty? By any professional standard he was far from being a failure.

He needed this leave; and an idyllic layover on the way home to Sol was a special bonus. Lately, even before the Hayashi incident, he had been feeling tired and stale.

He grinned abruptly at Brenda. "Enough about nightmares!" And he caught her by the arm and gently pulled.

"Oh, oh," said Brenda, gently chiding, and gently resisting. But her opposition was not very intense, and perhaps would not be too prolonged—

The communicator was chiming at them from under the dashboard of the little sportboat.

With a quick little gasp that sounded more like vexation than relief, Brenda suddenly exerted strength impressive for a young woman of her size and pulled away from him. "It must be important, or they wouldn't call."

She twisted around to touch a switch. "Brenda here. And Colonel Brazil. What's up?"

A male voice from the instrument at once began shouting at them, telling a confused story about a killing. Boris let the babble go on while he disengaged himself fully from Brenda and got the boat moving, away from the island and into open water. He steered carefully around a bend in the river, then accelerated downstream at the top thrust of the sporter's waterjets. A few kilometers ahead, he could see above the treetops the insubstantial-looking forcefield screens that were activated on occasion to shield the tiny colony of Earth-descended people.

Brenda, in shock over what the communicator was telling her, was silent. Boris put practiced calm into his voice as he answered it. "Is that you, Morton?" If Boris remembered correctly, Don Morton was the name of the colonist who happened to be presently standing the routine defensive watch. If any serious trouble had arisen, Morton might be forgiven a tendency to over-excitement. For ten years now there had been a colony of Earth-descended humans on this lonely, lovely planet called Kappa. Ten quite peaceful years, according to what Boris had heard about it, and no doubt by now the colonists were beginning to imagine that they understood the place.

"Yes, it's me. This is Don Morton. The defense tower."

"All right, fine. Now what's happened? This is Colonel Brazil. Start again, will you?"

"It's Jones." Morton's voice had regained some self-control. "He's gone crazy and killed a native. And now he's run away."

"Hang on. I'll be there in about two minutes."

Almost all that Boris knew about Edmund Jones
was that like himself the man was a planeteer, and
that he was spending a lengthy leave here on Kappa
pursuing an interest in anthropology that he said
was both professional and personal. Boris too was on
leave, but only stopping over, waiting for a ship that
would carry him home to Sol System.

Boris Brazil and Edmund Jones had started out a
few hours ago on a picnic with Brenda and Jane,
another currently unattached young woman of the
colony. But Jones had a standing request that he be
notified at once whenever a native medicine man
visited the colony, and so Morton had called Jones
on his boat radio about noon to tell him that a
shaman had arrived and was setting up camp near
the colony's main gate.

Certainly Jones had not been drunk or otherwise
deranged when, accompanied by a disappointed
Jane, he deserted the picnic and hurried back to see
the witch doctor. That gave him less than a standard
hour to somehow get in shape for craziness, killing,
and running away.

The sportboat skimmed the placid stream,
between shores covered with growth just a bit too
open and pleasant to be called jungle. Something in
the air and sun of Kappa gave to chlorophyll in
leaves a greener-than-reality travel advertisement
look. Had it been easier of access, the planet might
have more tourists and make an excellent site for a
big colony, thought Boris. As things were, dust
clouds and more or less permanent atomic storms
peppered the whole section of Galactic arm around
Kappa, making c-plus travel permanently

JANET AULISIO © 1980

uncertain.

Boris slowed the boat as it passed the riverside
landing field where shuttles came down from visiting
starships. The landing field was empty now. Just
ahead, the colony's defensive forcefield opened a
gate in itself at the place where it bulged out over
and into the river. Driving in through the gate, he
docked beside a rank of miscellaneous water craft.
Brenda stepped up to the dock beside him, and together they strode toward the defense tower. This
was a neglected-looking building four or five stories
high near the center of the small residential
compound. The compound contained only a couple
of dozen structures altogether, built mostly of glass
and native wood and stone, and inhabited by fewer
than three hundred Earth-descended people. The
colonists lived here, while automated machinery did
the routine work of running mines and farms and
ranches out in the zones of Kappa's grimmer
climates, where intelligent natives were few or none.

The Space Force, with its planeteers and research
teams, was gone from Kappa, moved on to worlds
yet unexplored. The colonists were people who liked
the life of an isolated small town, or they would not
have remained on Kappa long, maintaining a foothold for Earth, and making themselves comfortably
prosperous. Kappa had never offered them worse
than incidental and occasional danger.

But now Boris found half a dozen anxious people,
including Brenda's friend Jane, gathered in the
room that occupied the whole top level of the
defense tower. All were crowded around Morton's
sentry chair, watching his viewscreens.

Pete Kaleta, the colony's pudgy mayor, was speaking. "It all looks normal at the silver mine; he went in the other direction anyway. Oh, Brazil, very glad you're here."

"What's it all about?"

The colonists looked uncertainly at each other. When no one else seemed eager to speak, Jane began. "Jones—Eddie—hardly said a word all the way back here in the boat. But he didn't seem wild or anything. Just thoughtful."

Boris asked: "So what happened when he got here?"

Kaleta took a deep breath, and spoke. "A pair of men from a tribe just west of here arrived shortly after you four had left on your picnic. They started to set up camp just outside our main gate. One of them, a witch doctor by his face paint, said he wanted to see Jones—Jones has been talking to all the local witchmen. So Morton got Jones on the radio and Jones came back, put on a groundsuit, and walked out through the main gate."

"Put on a groundsuit?" asked Boris. "Why?"

Kaleta gestured nervously. "He didn't say. I suppose he wanted to impress the natives. Or maybe he just wanted to have the radio handy."

There were handier ways than putting on a suit, thought Boris, to carry a radio around.

The big viewscreen in front of the sentry chair now showed the area just outside the main gate. The grass there was littered with bright bits of fabric, scattered wooden boxes, and primitive utensils. In the foreground stood a native pack animal, grazing placidly. Heavy leather straps hung broken from its back; someone or something had torn the panniers from its sides and scattered the contents.

Don Morton, a powerfully-built young man, swung round in his sentry chair, and took up the story. "Jones went out there in the groundsuit and talked to the natives. I wasn't paying any particular attention to just what he said—I'm not even sure he had his suit radio on then." Morton looked at Boris belligerently, as if expecting to be accused of something.

"All right, go on."

When Morton hesitated, Jane said: "I came up here to watch, after Eddie told me he'd rather go out and talk to them alone. The first thing I saw was one of the Kappans outside offering Eddie a drink. He poured it from a funny kind of bottle—I've never seen one just like it before. And then Eddie did radio in. He said something like, 'Hey, better have a stomach pump ready, just in case.' He didn't drink whatever it was right away. He still had his helmet on, and was standing there talking to the witch doctor."

"Morton, I wish you'd called me," said Mayor Kaleta, staring into the viewscreen.

Morton shifted nervously in his chair. "Well, anyway, Jones sounded like he was serious about the stomach pump. So I called up the infirmary, and talked to Doc, here."

Doc pulled thoughtfully at a heavy mustache. "What that stuff was, I can't imagine. I wouldn't expect a small amount of any Kappan drink to have much effect on an Earthman—unless it was meant to be a poison. You know, Kappans and Earth-descended are remarkably similar in their biology, even for two prime-theme human races; I've seen experimental skin grafts made to take from one to the other. Anyway, as Morton says, I did get a stomach cleaner ready."

Morton took up the story again. "By the time I finished talking to Doc, Jones had his helmet off, and was starting to drink, from a little cup. He took a sip, and then he stood there talking for another minute; I don't know what about. Then he gulped the rest of the stuff down. Then, first thing I knew, he and the Kappans were arguing. I was just starting to pay closer attention when I guess he must have shut off his radio. I have no idea what the fight was about." Morton looked at Jane.

She said: "Well, I saw Eddie step forward, shouting at the Kappans. I guess he was threatening them. They backed away; they looked frightened and surprised."

"Jones grabbed at them," said Morton. "He knocked them down behind those bushes there. I think he must have killed them; you know the power in those suits. Then he tore the baskets off the pack animal and scattered all the stuff inside, as if he were looking for something. By that time I was already calling you and the mayor."

Mayor Kaleta seemed much worried. But he had nothing to say, for the moment.

"What kind of suit did Jones put on?" Boris asked.

"Heavy ground armor," Morton answered. "We keep two suits of it ready, just in case. We've never needed it."

"Ugh." It seemed to Boris that things just might

get much worse before they started getting better. He decided that he had better put on the other armored suit himself before going out to investigate.

Jane said: "And then Eddie found the bottle, where the Kappans had put it away, all wrapped up. He took another little drink, in a hurry, and then he set the bottle down in the grass as if it were something precious. Then he came back in through the gate."

"What?"

"Oh, yes." Morton had an angry look. "He radioed: 'Open up the outer gate, you fool, I need a rifle.' Well, I didn't know what the hell was going on. When he came back like that, I thought he must have some good reason. I mean, he's a planeteer, isn't he? He's supposed to know what he's doing in . . . in strange situations. Right?"

Boris said: "Well, let's find out how strange the situation is. So you opened the outer gate, and he came in again?"

"Right. And I opened the little door to the arms room, and he went in and got an energy rifle. We keep a couple of them handy, like the suits. And then he trotted off without another word, heading west."

Jane added: "And he picked up the odd little bottle and took it along with him."

The silent mayor had one hand over his eyes.

"I'd better get out there," said Boris. He adjourned the meeting to the arms room at the main gate, where he could get himself fitted into the remaining suit of heavy ground armor while the talk went on.

So, it seemed that Jones was running amok, with equipment that would make the average man as dangerous as a troop of saber-wielding cavalry. And Jones was not an average man, but a planeteer, with all the skills, including combat skills, of the professional interstellar explorer. Boris was a chief planeteer himself, when not on leave enjoying rest and recreation as he was now. So, it was quite logical for the colonists to call on him in an emergency like this one, and let him take over. Set one to catch one.

Possibly, he thought as he began cladding himself in armor, Jones is still rational. It's just that he's discovered something that makes it right for him to manhandle a couple of natives, arm himself even further, and then run off without a word of explanation. Boris couldn't imagine what such a discovery might be.

"Anything else peculiar around here? Unexplained?" he asked, while a couple of the colonists helped him with the fittings and fastenings of the armored suit.

"Things have been pretty dull," Kaleta said.

"Since Magnuson disappeared," said Doc. When Boris looked at him, he amplified: "An anthropologist, named Emanuel Magnuson. Used to work for the Space Force, spent most of his time out in the hills near Great Lake. He was supposed to leave when the last of the Space Force people pulled out, but instead he vanished. Looked like some carnivore probably got him."

"But you weren't sure?" Boris probed. "Could the Kappans have done him in?"

"We've always kept on good terms with them," said Mayor Kaleta, looking at Doc. "The Space Force seemed to be satisfied that Magnuson was killed by animals."

Doc, squatting to work on one of Boris's boots, contrived to shrug. "Maybe they were. He was a strange one. He'd argue his theories . . . there, how's that feel?"

"Okay." Boris brought an arm in from one suit sleeve and fastened his helmet from the inside. Then, checking his breathing apparatus as he went, he headed for the outer gate. For all the suit's weight and bulk, walking in it was easier than without it. Its limbs, powered by a tiny hydrogen fusion power lamp, were driven by servomechanisms that followed the movements of the wearer.

As he passed the door to the arms room Boris stepped in, took down the remaining energy rifle, and checked the charge. Such a weapon was effective at close range even against heavy ground-suit armor. If it should ever come to that.

When the main gate shimmered open for him, Boris went out and saw the scattered Kappan goods, and the grazing, phlegmatic animal. It would be nice, he thought, to find tracks indicating that the two Kappans had departed the area at a speed impossible for seriously injured men, and to find Jones sleeping off his strange intoxication behind a bush. Sometimes, Boris had noticed, the world was not nice.

Kappans were a leathery-skinned people, with very wide-set eyes and bulging foreheads, grotesque by Earthly standards of appearance. The first man

Boris found in the bushes was quite dead, with the insects at him already. The appearance of his head suggested that he might well have died of a blow from the power-driven arm of a groundsuit.

Boris's helmet radio brought him the collective gasp of the people in the defense tower; they were watching now through the television eye that rode on his shoulder.

"That's not the witch doctor," someone commented.

Boris turned up the sensitivity of his suit's air mikes and kept on searching, now holding the rifle ready with the safety off. When he had moved on a few more meters he caught the sound of ragged breathing. The second Kappan had crawled under a bush to hide. The wide-set eyes were open, and from behind oozing blood and witchman's paint they followed Boris.

"Send out a couple of stretcher bearers," he radioed. "And someone tell me a few soothing words to use."

Boris, helmet under one arm but still wearing the rest of the groundsuit, stood beside the hospital bed in which the injured Kappan lay. While Doc worked on the man, Brenda acted as translator.

"He says, just as soon as Jones had smacked his lips over the drink, he demanded to know where it came from. Jones was being initiated into the—well, the Kappan witch doctors' union, I guess you'd call it— so they told him the truth. It comes in trade from the western hill people, near the Great Lake. Then Jones demanded that they give him more of the drink, and when they wouldn't do that he went after

it. They tried to stop him from tearing up their
goods, but he just knocked them aside."

"What was in the drink?"

The Kappan hesitated for some time before giving
his short answer. Brenda glanced around at the
blank faces of the other colonists present, frowned,
and translated for Boris. "He says, 'The Water of
Thought.'"

"What's that mean?"

Everyone still looked blank. "I've never heard of
it," said Kaleta, who had just come into the
infirmary. "And I've been here eight years, always in
contact with the natives."

"Maybe this guy's making it up," said Morton,
shaking his head.

Boris said: "Well, an Earth-sized planet can hold
a lot of secrets. I'd be out of a job if it couldn't." He
drummed metal fingers on the helmet under his
arm. "You're all sure that there was nothing in the
Space Force reports about such a drink, or poison,
or whatever?"

Everyone nodded or murmured assent. "I can
check the memory banks," the mayor said. "But I'm
sure already. We practically memorized all those
reports."

"Then maybe this man *is* lying about it. Or it's
something new."

Brenda again questioned the Kappan, then
passed along his reply, which was fairly lengthy. "He
says it's old, very old. The Water of Thought lets a
man communicate with his animal ancestors; very
powerful medicine. He can tell us about it now, because we've saved his life. No one else has ever

reacted to it the way Jones did, he says; he says he guesses Earth-descended men are just different."

"If only Jones had remembered that simple fact," said Doc morosely. "Well, you people had better all clear out of here for a while. My patient needs some rest."

"Two anthropologists," said Boris, thinking aloud as he walked to the door of the infirmary. "One vanishes somewhere near this Great Lake, and the other is last seen running toward it. It is west of here, isn't it? Or is there more than one Great Lake?"

The colonists, most of them coming along with Boris, probed one another with the quick searching looks of people who have known one another for a long time.

"There's just one that I know about," said the mayor finally. "I don't see any connection, though, between what happened to Magnuson and what Jones is doing."

Brenda was keeping thoughtfully silent.

"Excellent man in his field, he was," said Morton, leading the way out into the sunlight. "Magnuson, I mean."

Time was passing, and Boris was in a hurry to get moving. But he had the feeling there was something relevant that he was not being told. "I've got to go after Jones. If any of you know anything that might help me, I'd better hear it."

Mayor Kaleta shrugged irritably. "We're telling you all we know, Brazil. No doubt you're right; someone must stop Jones, or there's no telling what he'll do, what problems he'll involve us in with the natives. Frankly I'm glad you're willing to take the risk of going after him. I don't want to send out a lot of untrained people, not knowing what he's up to with that suit and rifle, or what the natives might . . . " He looked back uncertainly toward the infirmary.

"You're right," Boris said. "Better keep your people here, inside the defenses, as much as possible. I'll need a copter and a pilot, though."

"Right. I'll see that a machine's ready." Kaleta hurried off.

"I'm as good a pilot as there is around," said Brenda.

II.

At an altitude of seven or eight hundred meters they had no trouble in following the trail that Jones had left. It ran as straight as some fanatical assassin's lunge, through bush and swamp and an occasional cultivated field, toward the western hills that were still eighty kilometers and more away.

Jones might be napping as he traveled, or unconscious, or even dead. The semi-robotic suit could be set to balance itself and walk, or even run at thirty kilometers an hour, holding to a course and steering itself around major obstacles. With its self-contained recycling systems and stock of emergency rations, it could keep a continuously sealed in wearer almost comfortable for a week, and functioning for a standard month.

Boris to his relief could see no signs along the trail that Jones had had any more trouble with the natives. Any Kappan who saw the suited figure pass would be likely to stay clear; Jones had knocked down rows of small trees that stood in his path.

"What do we do when we catch up with him?" Brenda asked cooly.

Boris reflected that he seemed to have made a

JANET AULISIO © 1980

good choice for pilot. "You set me down on his trail before then," he answered. "This copter makes too good a target for that rifle of his."

"You think he'd shoot us down?"

"We'd better think so." Boris watched Brenda's profile, which remained calm. Something about the behavior of the other colonists still bothered him, and he shot a sudden question: "What was this Emanuel Magnuson like?"

Brenda's eyes, watching the terrain and air ahead, were briefly clouded. "I think he was a fine man. He was good to Jane and me—in a fatherly sort of way. He was nice. But still there's something so—intense—about him."

"You speak as if you think he might be still alive."

"Do I? I guess I do. I get the impression sometimes —oh, I don't know."

"Tell me."

"It's like a feeling in the air, around the colony, that Dr. Magnuson didn't just die in a simple accident. Though I don't recall anything definite ever being said. Do you know what life in a small town's like? Or maybe our small town's unique."

"I was born in a small town. Under a dome on Mars. It's starting to puzzle me a little why you stay here, Brenda."

"Oh. When my parents died, I just stayed on. All the people are my family and friends. Jane and I are like the two orphans; maybe we're spoiled." She glanced over at Boris. "Sometimes I—we—get restless. We took a trip out once—"

Boris interrupted: "Better start down now. I don't think he can be more than six or eight klicks ahead of us. See that second meadow up there? Aim for it, but when you get about halfway there peel off sharply to the right. We'll take a little evasive action, just to be on the safe—"

The accustomed drone of the copter's engine had suddenly disappeared; in the heavy silence Boris looked overhead to see the jet-spun rotor idling toward a halt. In his stomach he felt the familiar start of free fall. His hands moved instinctively to the copter's controls, but Brenda's fingers were already there, doing the proper things.

But to no avail. The engine remained dead; Jones must have hit it squarely with a jolt from his energy rifle. The copter tilted forward, and forest replaced sky in front of Boris, ranks of trees coming closer in a long hard rush. The machine was not dropping quite like a rock, but neither could you describe what it was doing as a satisfactory glide.

"Bail out!" Boris yelled at Brenda. He reached to take what control was left out of her hands. "I've got the suit!"

Her fingers were already tightening the parachute straps over her coverall, but she hesitated momentarily, her wide brown eyes looking into his, checking in her own mind to make sure that what he said made sense. Then, just as Boris was about to shove her clear, she popped open the cabin door on her side and leaped out.

With metal arms he fought the controls until the steering column bent. And then the trees were upon him.

Bounce and bang. Bounce again, and smash. He held his arms before his faceplate, until he had

shocked and jolted to a halt. Blessed be heavy ground armor.

Boris's seat belt was holding him, upside down, among splintered branches. The copter was a mass of torn metal around him; no way that it was ever going to fly again. The afternoon sun beamed through a fine haze of leaves and sawdust, still drifting and settling.

Taking inventory of his sensations, Boris could find nothing worse than a couple of probable bruises. He began to break his way out of the wreckage. It had been a frustrating day, up to now, and there was a certain satisfaction in bashing aside obstructions. As soon as the way was clear, he undid his belt, hung for a moment by one arm, then dropped with a clanging thud to the ground. He retrieved his rifle, which had landed nearby, and saw with relief that it was undamaged—for all he knew, Jones might be coming round for another shot.

Now for Brenda. After getting his directions from the sun, Boris moved off through the forest at a fast lope, toward the area where he judged her parachute ought to have come down. After a few minutes of coursing back and forth he spotted the bright cloth spread on the ground.

"Boris!" Her voice came from above. She sat four meters high in a tree, clasping the shag-barked trunk. Her face was pale, but her voice was pretty good, all things considered. "My ankle's hurt. No, I'm all right, really; I climbed up here. I thought I might be able to see where you had come down."

"Well." Boris allowed himself a grin. "You can

relax now, your knight in shining alloy's here. If you're not injured it looks like we're in pretty good shape. Even if your ankle's hurting I can carry you back to the colony in five or six hours with this suit. Of course wearing the suit I won't enjoy the task nearly so much."

"What about Jones?" Brenda asked. "Are we just going to give up on finding him?"

"I was hoping you'd take that attitude. Just let me go check his trail, at least. He might be still nearby somewhere. Tell you what, suppose you come down from that tree and hide in a bush, and I'll call your name when I get back. My suit is number Two—see? I suppose that Jones must have on number One."

"Okay, go ahead. I'll be all right." Brenda started to get herself down from the tree. Boris observed that she was definitely favoring one leg.

There seemed little point in trying to tell her what to do if he didn't come back. So without further delay he moved out into the woods, slipping his bulk of metal along as quietly as possible. When he was out of Brenda's view he halted, waiting for a minute, watching to see if Jones would appear near her. Jones might have seen the chute come down, and he determined, for some mad reason, on more murder.

Jones did not materialize, and Boris soon moved on. Just about where he expected to find Jones's trail, he came upon it—a line of brush and saplings trampled down and bent toward the west. Evidently Jones still did now care a damn whether anyone was following him or not. Boris stayed with the trail for another hundred meters, and then noted hopefully that it had begun to waver. Soon it looped around as if the man making it were no longer sure of his directions.

And then Boris saw a silvery gleam ahead—Jones's suit, fallen on its faceplate in low grass. Boris let out a little sigh of relief, and moved forward, watching alertly—

"Freeze in your tracks, Brazil," said a voice not far behind him. "I've got a rifle on you."

There seemed to be little future in any other course.

"Now drop the rifle, and take off your helmet."

He did.

After a moment Jones came walking around to face him, well out of reach but easily close enough for the energy rifle he held to puncture Boris's armor. And the weapon stayed center-aimed at Boris.

Jones was almost as tall as Boris, and built more heavily. He sported a short black beard. More dark hair grew thickly on his bare massive forearms, and from the throat of his coverall. He looked happy.

"Well, what's the matter, Jones?" Boris asked. "I'd like to hear your side of this." He made his voice a trifle loud; it was conceivable that Brenda had now worked a cramp out of her leg and had decided to follow him.

Jones showed white teeth, and looked Boris's suit up and down with an expert eye. "No sidearms, eh? That's fine. Sit down against that tree over there, and I'll tell you my side, as you put it. Understand that I'll kill you, if need be, but I don't want to kill you. I've thought of a much better way."

"That's good to hear," said Boris, sitting down as

directed. Then he nodded toward Jones's fallen armor. "Neat ambush."

Jones ignored the compliment. "Brazil, I've tasted the Water of Thought—that's what the witchman said they call it. And I've come to know—" Jones paused, giving his head a little shake. "There's no use my trying to explain. I wouldn't have believed anyone who tried to tell me. You'll have to taste it yourself before you'll understand." Keeping an eye on Boris, he walked to the fallen groundsuit, and from somewhere inside it brought out what could only be the medicine man's bottle.

"No, now, wait, maybe I *can* understand," said Boris smoothly. "I'd like to try. You tore up those people's property back there and ran off, just to find more of this Water of Thought?"

"Tore up their property. I did more than that. I killed someone. Oh, I know that at least one of them is dead. But I had to do it, they were keeping me from the Water. You'll see when you taste it. Nothing could mean more to me now than it does; not food, or relief from pain, or women, or anything else. I sound like a madman, don't I? But you'll see how it is." Jones put a hand to his forehead. His face and eyes looked as if he might be developing a fever.

Boris thought rapidly. "Jones, do you have a family?"

"Never mind my family!" For the first time, though, Jones showed a hint of inner conflict. "I know I won't see them now for a long time. Maybe never. How can I, when the Water of Thought is here on Kappa?"

"All right, so it's necessary to get more of this

Water of Thought. Most likely it'll take a large expedition just to find out where the stuff comes from."

"Oh, no, Brazil." Jones chuckled. "No, you're not sweet-talking me back to the colony. They'd just stick me in the infirmary, and they wouldn't give me any more Thought-Water if they had any, which they don't. Right now, the only way I can get along with another Earthman is to convert him to my way of thinking." So saying, Jones held up his stone bottle. "You will be my first disciple."

Keep him talking, thought Boris. Maybe the stuff will wear off, or he'll pass out. "Jones, are you religious?"

Jones accepted the question as relevant. "You know, I wasn't."

"And now you are? I don't understand."

"Of course you don't. But you will. You will." Still keeping the rifle steady, Jones used his teeth to loosen the carved top of the bottle. Removed, it made a little drinking cup. He set the cup down on a level spot of ground and very carefully poured it half full of clear liquid from the bottle.

"This is God, Brazil. That's what I mean. God's in my little bottle here." It was only with great evident effort that Jones was able to keep from drinking the contents of the cup himself. But he backed away from it, still holding the bottle and the rifle. "Now drink that!" he ordered. "Move forward slowly and drink it."

"If I take any, there'll be less for you."

Jones bit his lip. "It's an investment, to get more. That's the only reason I can stand to give it away. One man alone can always be tricked or trapped somehow, but with two of us, in ground armor, working together, the Kappans will never be able to keep us from getting at the source of the Water. Now drink! I'm in a hurry. If I must, I'll kill you and go on alone."

Boris stood up slowly, and walked slowly forward; he had heard the sincere intent of murder before, and recognized it now. But experience gave no protection against the cutting edge of fear.

"Just let me walk away, Jones," he said loudly. "Even without my groundsuit. I could just walk back to the colony." Possibly Brenda was listening, wondering what to do, and would accept the hint. "It would take me a couple of days, and you'd get away."

Jones only moved the rifle muzzle slightly, motioning toward the cup. It would be plain suicide to try to rush Jones. Swallowing the Water of Thought might be suicide of a different kind, but it seemed to Boris that if he drank he would at least keep on breathing. And while breath lasted, there was always hope. Three or four days should see the arrival in Kappan orbit of the cruiser that Boris had been expecting to ride home to Sol; the cruiser would have the people and the equipment to mount a massive search.

Boris decided to try one last argument. "Jones, I—"

"One more stalling word and you're dead."

Boris bent down, reaching for the cup. He noticed that his fingers were still steady. As if that meant anything.

"Brazil, if you spill even one drop, I'll take the

time to kill you slowly, before I go on."

Carefully, Boris picked up the cup. The liquid in it was as clear and thin as spring water, or raw corn whisky. A subtle, slightly fishy odor rose from it.

"Drink!"

As a man threatened with drowning would clutch for physical support, so Boris tried to clamp a mental hold on sanity. He hoped that Brenda would somehow know enough to run from him if he went mad. The fluid in the cup rose before his face, a tidal wave to sweep his mind away. I am the master of my fate—

"Drink!"

Boris sipped. The stuff had an alien tang, not unpleasant, but with a ghost of fishiness. He swallowed the half-cupful of the Water of Thought, and found it pleasantly cooling to his throat.

Boris brought his hand down with the empty cup in it, being careful not to spill a single drop. He tried to brace his mind against the overwhelming lust for another drink, that any second now must strike.

Jones relaxed, sure of himself now, slinging the rifle over his shoulder. "Brazil, I'll pour you another little shot, if you like. Share and share alike with this bottle. You don't have to rush me for it. It might spill, and we wouldn't want that, would we?" His chuckle had an obscene sound.

Boris felt a moment of mental confusion; but it seemed to pass. He still had no craving for the Water of Thought. Could he hope to be immune? He would play along with Jones, hold out the cup as if demanding another drink, and as soon as Jones had poured it Boris would throw down the cup and grab—

And then Boris discovered that he was unable to move a muscle.

He still breathed, and obviously his heart was still beating. He didn't feel numb. But he couldn't move. He felt sweat break out on his forehead.

Jones stepped closer to him. "What's the matter with you? Brazil. Look at me. Answer me!"

As if with a life of their own, Boris's eyes swiveled obediently to look at Jones. Boris's voice, speaking without his volition, said: "The matter with me is I can't move."

"Hah!" said Jones, an incredulous snort.

"So, you can't move without being ordered," said Jones, three minutes later, pacing back and forth. "You can't be faking. If you were faking, you'd pretend to feel the way I do. I'd have fallen for that. Then you'd take me by surprise, and drag me back to the colony." Jones shuddered. "They'd keep me there, alive, but without the Water. They'd try to *cure* me."

With a quick move Jones grabbed the empty cup from Boris's statue-hand, tilted the bottle again, and rationed himself a tiny drink. He swallowed it, gasped, and stood for a moment with his eyes closed. Then he carefully capped up the bottle again. "Oh, put your arm down," he said in preoccupied annoyance.

Boris's arm relaxed. But the rest of his body remained frozen, save for his eyes. They still helplessly followed Jones, who had begun to pace again.

"You don't have to watch me all the time!" Jones

barked. Then, in an apologetic tone, he added: "Look—you can stand easy, or whatever you want to call it. Just don't try to attack me, or run away, or disobey me—or communicate with the colony. Outside of that you can move any way you like. All right?"

Boris's neural circuits seemed to close again.

"I guess it'll have to do," he said. The paralysis had left him so shaky that he sat down and closed his eyes. He hoped that Brenda was hiking toward the colony by this time. Probably, though, she would spend the approaching night in a tree somewhere near here. And it seemed likely that the colonists would come searching out this way in the morning, and spot her parachute and the copter wreckage. Boris wished he knew more about Mayor Kaleta and the other people back at the colony.

"Well, maybe this is all right!" said Jones, suddenly pleased. "Yes, I think so. You'll have to help me, and when we find more of the Thought-Water I won't have to share it with you."

Opening his eyes, Boris saw Jones climbing cheerfully back into his groundsuit. If Boris moved quickly, he could beat Jones to one of the rifles. Boris decided to leap for the weapon, grab it up, and kill Jones if need be. Boris decided to do it, but that was as far as he could get. His body would not even consider a translation of the plan into action.

At least, he thought, I still have my sanity, upon which I took so tight a grip. But what good is sanity to me now? And how long will it last?

Jones resumed his westward march. By his order,

Boris walked beside him. I am a semi-robotic man, Boris thought, walking inside a semi-robotic suit. that adds up to one whole robot, plus a little extra machinery. Plus a little something else, all that is left of me. Or might the little bit of something else be an illusion?

Darkness found them on the first slopes of the western hills, and there Jones called a halt. Ahead lay hundreds of thousands of square kilometers of rough, forest-covered country, almost completely unexplored.

"There'll be more copters out looking for us, sooner or later," said Jones, turning his faceplate up to the first stars of the night. "So we'll light no fire. And we'll take turns standing watch, just in case. Wake me in two hours, or sooner if you see or hear anything I'd want to know about."

So Jones lay down to sleep; and Boris found himself unable to do anything but stand guard against those who might be coming to rescue him.

At first, the passage of time gave him some hope. The effects of any drug would surely wear off, sooner or later. Probably, he thought, in a matter of no more than hours. But two hours passed, and then he had no choice but to awaken Jones. Then Boris, on command, lay down and drifted off into a daze of sickly dreams, bad dreams, in which he was compelled to fight with a child's thin arms against an overwhelming faceless Something—

Jones was shaking his suit to awaken him. Jones had been on watch for more than two hours, for it was almost dawn. Twenty meters or so away a figure was standing motionless, partially hidden by the thick morning mist.

It's a man, was Boris's first thought, it's a short Kappan savage without clothes. The apparition was at least a head shorter than Boris, male, with grayish leathery skin and a heavy growth of dark hair at crotch and armpits, on the forearms and lower legs. The overall configuration was undoubtedly prime theme.

Standing up slowly, with his open hands spread out, Jones made the planeteers' basic gesture for greeting primitive prime theme people. With a bobbing, somehow apelike motion of its upper body, the figure half-turned away from Boris and Jones. It hesitated in that attitude, as if on the verge of flight but looking back over a shoulder at the two men. Its arms were muscular, but short, not apelike. Boris imagined he saw intelligence in the pale eyes, and then imagined he saw the lack of it. Jones gestured again, and the creature turned and sped away into the mist, running easily, like a man.

"So," said Jones, in a tone suggesting that he was not greatly surprised. "The Kappan hominid does exist. It was carrying something in one hand."

"Yes. I believe it had a rock." So might Earth's first tool-maker have looked, Boris thought, a few million years ago. "You'd say that it *was* pre-human, then?"

"Wouldn't want to stake my life on it." Briefly Jones had become a planeteer again. "The survey missed the hominids completely. Only in the last couple of years a few stories have leaked out of these hills. The other Kappans who live in this area call the hominids the Forest People."

"Our survey missed a whole species? A large, mammalian species at that?"

Jones removed his helmet and rubbed his neck. He looked tired, but no longer particularly feverish. "Sounds like sloppy work, sure. But just look at this country around here; you can see how it'd be easy to miss a lot. High-crowned forest, very difficult to see under it."

"That's true."

"What we just saw looked a lot like a Kappan human. But the hominids in my opinion are probably a separate species." Then Jones grew distracted, surveying the morning sky. "The trees will help to hide us, too—we'll need that." He picked up his energy rifle and adjusted the vernier for a fine beam. "Think I'll take a little walk, scout around, and try to get us some meat for breakfast. Why don't you get a small fire started?"

Boris got to his feet and automatically began to look around for usable wood. "That was a neat shot that you made yesterday."

Jones looked blank. "What?"

"Hitting my copter."

Jones blinked. "I never saw your copter after it started down. Didn't you just land it?"

III.

Brenda was awakened from uneasy sleep by the sound of a copter's rotors. She had dozed off in spite of everything, after tying herself into the crotch of a tree five meters up, a tactic she thought likely to foil any of the local predators with which she was more or less familiar. The sun was barely up now, burning away a low ground mist. Above the mist the greenish sky was clear.

The copter was circling slowly, a hundred meters or so above her head. Before climbing this tree she had managed to spread the bright cloth of her parachute to its widest stretch, making a marker visible a long way off.

Brenda waved energetically. The copter circled once more, then started down to land a little distance off, where trees were thinner. She unknotted the belt with which she had secured herself to the tree, and started to climb down. Sharp pain awoke in her right ankle whenever she put weight on it, and she could feel that it was swollen above her low-cut shoe. Should have worn boots.

When she reached the ground, she remained where she was, clinging to the tree trunk. Presently

JANET AULISIO © 1980

Kaleta appeared, coming toward her from the direction of the landed copter. The mayor was carrying a machine pistol, and he looked around him warily.

"Mayor Pete! Am I glad to see you!"

Something was wrong about the way the mayor looked at her. "Where's Brazil?" he asked.

"He went on chasing after Jones, yesterday before dark. Boris said he'd come back in a few minutes, but he never did. I was worried, but I couldn't go looking for him—my ankle's hurt. Something's happened to him, and we've got to get more people out here and start searching, right away."

"Hm. We've got to find him, all right. Here, if you can't walk, lean on me." They started toward the mayor's copter.

"I'm sorry, Brenda," the mayor said, watching her limp as they drew near the machine. "I didn't intend—well, now you're in this, I suppose. There's nothing to be done about it."

"What's up?" Don Morton demanded, leaning from the pilot's seat of the copter. Jane, looking small and frightened, sat beside him.

"Brazil's gone west, I guess," said Kaleta, motioning in that direction with his gun. "After Jones, or with him."

"I don't like it." Morton shut off the copter's idling engine and hopped out. "Why couldn't we have had a couple more energy rifles?" he complained to the world at large. He slapped his own holstered pistol. "I don't know about one of these things—against those suits."

"Are you going to call for help?" Brenda demanded, trying to cope with growing astonishment.

"No," said Don Morton. "Shut up and get in the back seat."

Brenda had seen Morton in ugly moods before, but this looked like the worst. She kept quiet for the moment, and climbed up into the rear of the copter. Jane gave her a hand up, and then sat beside her. The men moved away a little, talking to each other in low, urgent voices.

"What's going on?" Brenda whispered.

Jane was near tears. "Oh, Brenda, honey, I'm sorry. I knew Don and Mayor Pete were up to something. I guess I knew it was smuggling. But I didn't know that crazy business yesterday had any connection with it. And there I was, telling everyone just what Eddie did outside the gate, before Don could hush me up. I thought he was going to kill me, later."

"Smuggling? Smuggling what?"

"That—damned drink. It's some kind of drug . . ." Jane bowed her face into her hands.

Right now, to Brenda, the most pressing thing was still that Boris needed help. Intending to call the colony herself, she reached forward to the copter's radio—and found that all power was off, not to be restored by pressing switches.

She leaned out of the cabin. "Please, Mayor Pete! Don!"

The mayor would not meet her eye. And Don Morton held up the copter's power key, showing her that he had it. His smile was ugly indeed. "Just behave," he said. "The good mayor and I are going to do our own searching. In our own good time."

"You're not drinking much from your bottle," Boris commented, when he and Jones were on their way again, striding up a long slope through open forest. After a breakfast of roast meat, Jones had taken a single swallow of the Water of Thought; he had otherwise been content with the ordinary water in his suit's canteen unit.

"I know something about drug addiction." Jones smiled faintly behind his faceplate. "This is something different from any addiction I've ever heard of. In fact I'm not an addict, in the sense that I don't suffer physically from abstaining.

"No, the effect seems almost purely—mental. I can't describe it. I don't think that any doctor could —or any poet. All I know is that nothing else will matter to me, for the rest of my life."

"How did you come to take the first drink?" Boris asked, and felt the ghost of humor at sounding like someone interviewing an old alcoholic.

"Why, I wanted to get in good with the witchmen." Jones laughed without humor. "I told you I know something about drug addiction. I'm here on Kappa for Space Force Intelligence. The crime syndicate's taken an interest in this planet lately, and we've wondered about the attraction. Some kind of exotic dope seemed like a good bet, but I swallowed the stuff before I knew I'd found it. And once I'd swallowed it I wasn't about to try any of the possible antidotes available. All I really wanted from the witchmen was information about the tribes up in these hills, and to try to get a line on Magnuson. He seems to be involved somehow, that story about his being eaten by predators was never very convincing."

"He worked for the Space Force too, didn't he?"

"Yes. Toward the end he seems to have spent most of his time arguing with his boss. There was research he wasn't being allowed to carry out; it seems he wanted to make anthropology an experimental science. He had theories about reinforcing natural selection, weeding out the unfit. Of course the Tribunes vetoed any such scheme."

"So you think he went into hiding here, to work in secret?"

"That's what SFI thought when they sent me. Now, I think he might have tasted the Water too." Jones looked at Boris. "It's hit you one way and me another. There's no telling what it might have done to him."

In the afternoon Boris and Jones passed four Kappans, who stood in a group at some distance, watching them. These were not hominids, but tall spear-carrying warriors who closely resembled the men of the tribes nearer the colony and were certainly of the same species. Jones waved at them in passing, but when he got no reply did not attempt a closer approach.

"They don't seem too surprised by our suits," observed Jones thoughtfully. "Evidently they've had some contact with colonists. Maybe with Magnuson."

"So, what do we do now?"

"For now we just walk on some more. Let ourselves be seen."

At sunset Boris and Jones dined again on fresh-killed meat. And again Boris was assigned the first watch after dark.

He had not asked a second time for his freedom. It was not something to be given him, but something to take when he was able.

He would try now, with all the will that he could muster. Jones slept, stretched out beside the little fire, whose flickering light made ancient armor of his suit.

Boris picked up a rifle. Experimentally, he tried to aim the weapon at Jones, and found that he could not. There was nothing that could be described as a struggle with himself; it was simply that his hands and arms refused to make the required motions.

At last he threw the rifle down, and looked up through the treetops at the stars. Killing Jones, or threatening him, was not really the answer anyway. The trouble was inside himself.

Boris faced in the proper direction, back toward the colony, and drew a deep breath. He willed himself to walk quietly away. But his feet would not move. After a long time he sat down.

Again Jones's shaking awakened Boris to a cool and misty dawn. What had looked in the evening twilight like another valley about a kilometer distant Boris now saw to be a lake, at least six or eight kilometers wide. Much of its extent was obscured by patches of morning haze.

Eight Kappan men, armed with spears and wearing loincloths, stood about twenty meters off, watching the two Earthmen stolidly. The visitors were obviously not much impressed by groundsuits.

When he saw that Boris was awake Jones slowly stood up, making the peace gesture. Boris imitated him, without being ordered. He welcomed the appearance of the natives, on the theory that his predicament was so bad that any random change was likely to be for the better.

Some of the Kappans imitated the peace gesture. Others conferred among themselves. At last the tallest one stepped forward and spoke, clearly, in the language of Earth's colonies and Space Force: "You men of Earth, why do you walk here?" He had an odd accent, but Boris had understood worse.

Jones answered: "We are looking for another Earthman, called Magnuson. We are the enemies of his enemies, so we want to be his friends."

The tall warrior looked them over for another minute. Then he raised one arm, as if waving to someone a considerable distance away. "Wait," he said. "Magnuson is not far. But if you try to use your far-speakers, he will hear them. And then you will not find him."

"We will wait," said Jones. He turned to Boris. "If Magnuson has radio equipment out here, it means that he's been getting help."

Boris came to a decision. "Jones, I don't think you're my worst enemy on this planet. I'd better tell you something. You know that accidental failure of one of these copters is very unlikely. If you didn't shoot at mine, then someone probably sabotaged it."

"So. Probably our smuggler didn't want you to catch me. Wants us both out of the way. Who do you think it was?"

"Probably the mayor. Another thing—Brenda was with me in the copter, and she had to parachute. She's back there somewhere with a twisted ankle. I didn't want to tell you when I thought you were wildly murderous."

Jones turned away, then back. "If she's in trouble, I'm sorry about it. But if my own family means nothing to me now, then how much do you suppose Brenda means?"

The two Earthmen waited, not looking at each other for a while. The warriors still leaned on their spears, watching impassively. Perhaps half a standard hour passed, and the mist lifted slowly into the greenish sky, revealing most of the lake's shoreline. Two or three kilometers away, set back a little from the shore, the huts of a village slowly became visible. The settlement straddled the mouth of a small river and was almost concealed under the forest's edge.

In the direction of the village, but much closer, another Kappan warrior suddenly appeared on a hillock, waving his arms.

"Walk," said the tallest warrior, the one who had spoken in Earth-colonial. He had circles of red paint or clay that Boris was later to learn denoted both his name and his rank daubed round his thick arms, and his flint-bladed spear was longer by two handspans than any of those of the men with him. Now he motioned with it toward the distant village. Jones and Boris started in that direction; the Kappans followed.

Coming closer to the village, Boris was mildly sur-

prised to see how well built it was, with an air of
permanence. The houses—you could hardly call
them huts—were of dressed logs and shingles, a few
even of stone, and stone paths neatly connected
them. There was a central building, larger than the
rest, which appeared to be a temple of some kind. It
was constructed half of smooth-cut stone, half of
elaborately carved wood. Boris was certain that
other villages of the same or tributary tribes must be
nearby; there were not enough dwellings visible here
to support the social superstructure that was implied
by the temple.

It was quite possible that the Space Force survey,
done ten years before, had not even touched these
people. The whole planet would of course have been
mapped by aerial and orbital photography, but
ninety-five percent of the surface could have
received no more attention than that.

A little mob of village children promptly formed
as men and women came out of the houses. They
seemed to be no more than calmly curious as Jones
and Boris drew near. The people of this village wore
robe-like garments, and their gestures were gentle.
They were of the same stock as the eight hard-
muscled warriors, but obviously of some different
class or caste.

The tall spearman with the red-circled arms now
came to the front of the procession to lead Jones and
Boris through the village. Boris's planeteering eye
judged that the warriors were not conquerors here,
for they moved courteously enough among the soft-
robed people.

Spanning twenty meters of quiet river, a wooden

bridge thumped and squeaked under the booted weight of groundsuits. Just ahead was the temple building, and now in its doorway there appeared a lean and shaggy Earthman, dressed in worn coverall and boots. He had the bearing of a leader, and the robed villagers who were near made way for him deferentially.

Jones halted a few paces from the temple doorway, and made its occupant a slight bow. "Dr. Magnuson. I'm glad to meet you at last."

The man returned the nod almost casually. He was casting quick, appraising glances over Jones and Boris. "Gentlemen, you puzzle me," he announced in a cool, detached voice. Boris felt that the tone contained an assumption of superiority. "You've been walking for at least a day in this area, but you've made no radio contact with the colony."

"Magnuson, they say that your enemies are theirs also," the tall warrior informed him.

Jones smiled. "That's right, Doctor. I've come to prefer your way of life."

Boris thought that the appraising eyes were puzzled by this. But they turned calmly enough to him. "And you, sir?"

"He's drugged," Jones cut in. "Never mind about him for the moment. Magnuson, I want to speak to you alone, right away. It's urgent."

"Why not? Come inside and we can talk." Magnuson gestured toward the entrance to the temple.

Boris, compelled by a quick nod, followed Jones inside; Magnuson came in after them. The interior was dim, divided into several rooms, and held nothing immediately startling to an experienced planeteer's eye. A couple of the soft-robed people were there. Magnuson said a few words to them, and after hesitating for a moment they made graceful gestures and went out.

Magnuson turned to Jones. "Very well. What is it?"

"I want the source of the Water of Thought," said Jones in a deliberate voice. "And I want it right away."

"So." Magnuson hesitated thoughtfully. "Once I wanted very much to find that myself. I should still like to, but . . . may I ask what your reason is for wanting it?"

"I don't want to steal it, or smuggle it offworld. I just want some for myself. I could agree to any of a number of different arrangements, provided I'm guaranteed a steady supply. A few mouthfuls a day would be enough. But that much I mean to have, make no mistakes. I've already killed men for the Water. You know the power in these suits?"

"I'm not a fool," said Magnuson shortly. Boris thought he was more offended than worried by Jones's demand.

Magnuson went on: "Some of the Water of Thought is available, right here in this village. I'll undertake to guarantee the amount you say you need. Provided that you work with me."

"Where does it come from?"

"The warriors make periodic raids into territory upstream along the Yunoee—that's the river running through the village. They capture the Water somewhere up there, and bring it back with them in pails." Magnuson gestured at some containers stacked against a wall. "I don't really know any more than that. I've made myself a person of some importance here, as you'll see, but I'm still not privy to the tribal secrets. In fact I am in some ways a dictator, yet I am still not a full member of the people. Perhaps I shall be, soon." He smiled suddenly, with surprising magnetism.

Jones was looking about. "You say there's some of the Water here in the village? Show me."

Magnuson's brow creased in a small frown. "Remember, it's a sacred thing to these people."

"Show me."

Magnuson hesitated briefly. "All right. Come this way." He led them behind a stone altar, and through a door into another room. This was a windowless place, lighted only by a few oil lamps on low stone pedestals. Half a dozen of the robed men were here; two of them lay supine on a mat of woven branches, and Boris was not sure that those two breathed.

"They've drunk the Water of Thought," said Magnuson, indicating the two men on the mat. "Kappans claim to experience racial memories under its influence."

It seemed to be all things to all men, thought Boris. He found himself able to speak up. "What did it do to you, Doctor?"

Magnuson's vital eyes flicked at him. "Nothing of importance."

"Where is it?" Jones demanded.

Magnuson bent down. From the floor near one side of the room he lifted another woven mat, and then a tight-fitting hardwood cover. A sunken bathtub-sized vat was revealed. The liquid in the vat looked black in the dim light.

Jones took a step forward, peering at it. "You mean, that whole tubful is—the Water?"

"Yes. The priests here try to keep a stock—what are you doing?"

Jones had dropped to his knees beside the sunken vat. He pulled his helmet off and tossed it aside. Turning to Boris then, he ordered: "Brazil, watch them. If any of them starts to do anything dangerous to me, kill him. Say you'll obey me."

Boris's hands moved to unsling his rifle, and his finger flicked the safety off. His chest forced air up through his throat, and his throat and his mouth made a word out of it: "Yes."

Jones bent over the vat, and there was a stir among the watching Kappans. Magnuson gestured sharply, and said something; the robed ones muttered but stood still.

Jones dipped a finger into the vat, then raised it to his mouth, tasting. A moment later he had stretched himself out prone on the stone floor, and was thrusting down his head to drink.

Boris had to watch Magnuson and the Kappans, to see if they might be going to do anything dangerous to Jones: To judge by their faces they were not pleased at what was happening. There was a bubbling sound; Boris wondered what his own fate was going to be if his master drowned himself.

At last there came a louder gurgle, followed by a gasp, and Boris was able to look down. Jones was rolling over on the floor, his armor clanking on

stone. His whole head was wet, and his eyes moved
like a baby's, chasing things unseen by others. For
an instant Boris thought that the man had been
poisoned, but then he saw that Jone's ecstasy was of
pleasure and not of pain.

Jones cracked the stone floor with a metal fist.
"Brazil, let them kill me if they want to!" But a
moment later he thought better of that order, and
sat up. "No, don't let them! I can drink again tomorrow, and the day after, and every day, for years
and years." As if his body were a new and unfamiliar
thing, Jones got unsteadily to his feet, and leaned for
support against a carven temple post.

An oil lamp sputtered. Everyone else in the room
was silent, while Jones's gasping breath slowly
returned to normal.

His eyes came back at last to look at the others. To
Magnuson he said: "There's plenty of the stuff here
for both of us. We have no quarrel."

Magnuson was as coldly controlled as before. "I
don't use the drug. And you are forgetting those who
do, the owners. My friends here will not allow you
unlimited wallowing in that vat. No. I told you it
was sacred to them."

"We'll see about that."

"Oh, I don't doubt that in those suits you could
destroy this village. But doing that won't help you
find the source of the Water. Not if you kill the
whole tribe."

Jones let go of his support. "I don't want any more
killing. But I'll do anything to find that source."

Magnuson moved two paces away, and stood for a
moment with his back to everyone. Then he spun

JANET AULISIO © 1980

around. "You say you'll do anything. Will you join this tribe? I'm supposed to be initiated into it soon. The ceremony can be moved up, held a day or two from now."

"What'll I gain by doing that?"

"More than you know." Again, that sudden, magnetic smile. "Once initiated, we will be entitled to know all the tribal secrets. And these people will help and defend us like brothers."

Jones thought it over. "Might be a good idea at that."

Magnuson nodded. "I'll explain the details presently. But right now, things will be easier if you'll leave the temple."

Jones delayed, looking down at the Water of Thought in its dark vat. "Funny. Now, when I try to imagine the source, I can almost see . . . a green, peaceful place. But it's like—like trying to recall a dream that's almost slipped away." Abstractedly, shaking his head, he moved to the door and out of the room.

Magnuson shook his head also, looking after Jones. "It's not good that he should drink so much of it." Then he put a hand on Boris's suited arm. "You must follow his orders?"

"That's right."

"When did you first drink the Water of Thought —both of you?"

Boris thought back. It seemed like a year. "This is the third day."

"I drank the Water once myself, and in five days its effects had left me. I offer you this hope now; and I trust you'll remember me when I in turn need help."

Boris could not let himself start hoping very hard. "What did it do to you, Magnuson? What was the effect that passed away in five days?"

"I told you it was nothing of importance. But that isn't really true; the Water brought me here." Magnuson looked round the temple. "To more important things than drugs." The smile flashed. "Come. You are both my guests tonight, and we are going to have a feast."

IV.

The calm water of Great Lake mirrored the greenish sunset. In front of Magnuson's hut, or house, torches were set up on poles and lighted. A low table was brought from somewhere, and platters of food prepared. Acting as cooks and waiters and furniture-movers were Kappans who wore neither the warrior's loincloth or the priests' robes, but a kind of kilt. The kilted workers, men and women alike, wore their hair in long braids.

Emerging from his dwelling, Magnuson addressed Jones cheerfully. "I would suggest that you and Brazil get out of those suits, if you want the people here to accept you. You'll certainly have to remove the helmets if you're going to share their food."

"All right, we can't live sealed in forever." Jones's eyes were still distant, and his face had a feverish look again. He had spent most of the day after his drink sitting alone, as if preoccupied with thought. "Let's relax for a while, Brazil."

A minute later, the empty suits lay with the rifles on the ground. Five seconds after that, the necks of Boris and Jones were each ringed by half a dozen spearpoints. Boris, at least, was not greatly

surprised.

Magnuson was pleased, but also worried. He chided the spearmen in their own language, and pulled gently at their arms. The rings of flinty points widened by a few centimeters.

"I'm sorry to frighten you," said Magnuson, sounding sincere. "Still, my Kappan friends here have the right idea. You must be subject to my plans, not I to yours. A great deal more than your lives or mine is at stake here. Humanity itself. Yes."

Red Circles, who Boris had decided was probably chief of all the warriors, appeared, and smiled to see the groundsuits and rifles already separated from their owners. Red Circles held a brief dialogue with Magnuson, then issued a few sharp orders. The ring of threatening spears dissolved. Teams of kilted workers carried away the suits and rifles.

Magnuson excused himself briefly. "I have a short radio message to send, and I'd better do it before nightfall. There are nocturnal atmospheric changes, as you doubtless know, that can make radio privacy harder to maintain." He paused, nodding to his prisoners. "Soon enough, the colony and the galaxy will know where I am and what I'm doing. But not just yet." He turned and went into his house.

Jones looked round. A couple of spearmen at a little distance were watching. "Brazil," he said. "I'm sorry."

"That we've lost our suits? I don't think I am."

"I mean sorry about compelling you to help me. But then I didn't really have any choice."

"I know how that goes," Boris said.

In a minute, Magnuson had rejoined them.

"Gentlemen, shall we dine?" He motioned them to places at the low table. "Sit down. Relax. Believe me, I mean you no harm. No. There is suffering enough."

With a slave's fatalism, Boris squatted on a mat and began to eat. He was just getting a good start on his portion of roast meat when he heard the sound of an approaching copter.

Beside him, Jones jumped to his feet, shouting: "Our suits! Quick! Bring them back!"

But Magnuson, showing no great excitement, simply stood up from the table and walked away, motioning his two guests to remain where they were. The copter's sound grew louder in the darkness, slowed, and then died abruptly, as if the machine might have made a radar landing nearby. In a few minutes Magnuson was back, and Boris was not much astonished to see Pete Kaleta, a pistol strapped on his hip, walking beside him. Don Morton and Jane were a little more of a surprise; and then, provoking an unexpectedly sharp reaction in Boris, Brenda walked into the firelight. Her hands were behind her as if they might be tied, and she was limping rather badly, but she appeared otherwise unhurt. The relief in her eyes when they discovered Boris tore at the raw wound of his helplessness.

Kaleta stopped in front of him. "I meant you no harm, Brazil. Or Brenda. I didn't expect your copter would fail quite so suddenly. I'm no expert at sabotage."

"No one on this planet has yet meant me any harm," said Boris. "How far behind you is the Space

Force?"

"I meant I wasn't trying to kill you." The mayor
stared thoughtfully at Boris; the past tense hung in
the air; the stare was all the worse in that it did not
seem intended to frighten.

Magnuson suddenly noticed Brenda's bound
hands. He yanked a knife from a sheath at his belt
and cut her free. "There's no need for this damnable
business!" He hurled pieces of cord away.

"Who said you could—" Morton's move toward
Magnuson was stopped by Red Circles' spear leveled
at his chest. Morton took a step back, his hand going
to the holster at his side.

"No!" Kaleta grabbed at Morton. "Take it easy.
We can't afford—take it easy, will you? We'll talk
this over later."

There was a little silence. Morton, glowering, at
last relaxed a little.

"Go ahead, tough guy," said Jane to him at last.
"Get us all killed." With a little shudder she moved
away from him, toward the table. "I see supper's
ready. Are we all invited?"

"You are indeed," said Magnuson. He looked big,
standing protectively beside little Brenda. Beside
him she looked very young. She rubbed her freed
hands, her brown hair hanging loose around her
face.

"Thank you," she said to Magnuson. Then she
looked across the table at Boris. "Are you all right?
Our *mayor* came and *rescued* me this morning, as
you see."

"I'm alive; I'm drugged," Boris told her. Her eyes
went wide.

Magnuson sheathed his knife. "Let's all have something to eat," he advised calmly. "Then we can talk."

While eating, Boris kept a planeteer's eye turned on the Kappans. None of them were sharing Magnuson's table tonight, yet Boris got the impression that they might be at the next meal. Their relationship with Magnuson was undoubtedly complex; the robed priests deferred to him, the warriors defended him and took his orders about some things at least, and the kilted workers served him. Yet he had said that they would not tell him the secret of the source of the Water of Thought; not that he now seemed to be very much interested in finding out . . .

Brenda from her seat across the table was silently appealing to Boris for reassurance if not active help. He found himself resenting the way that she was looking at him. He wanted to scream at Brenda that he was more helpless than she was, that there was nothing he could do for her, not a thing, whatever happened. With an effort he kept his face calm, kept himself from screaming; that was about all that he could do.

Jane was a frightened young woman, and showed it, eating almost nothing, looking from one face to another for some sign of hope.

Kaleta and Morton and Jones were all dining in poker-faced silence.

Even now, relaxed, Magnuson still had the bearing of a chief. He ate sparingly, though with evident enjoyment. At last he wiped greasy fingers on a cloth handed him by a kilted worker-girl, and belched with healthy satisfaction. The worker-chef, standing nearby, smiled at this sign of approval.

"On Kappa," Magnuson began the conversation, "Eden is here and now."

At Boris's side, Jones raised his head. He turned his face, with an odd expression, down the table toward Magnuson.

Magnuson gestured at the villagers nearby. "Oh, for these people, and for the rest of their species scattered round the planet, Eden of course has passed. But nevertheless, for some other creatures in the wilderness near here, its time is now."

The Kappan night was deep around the little torch-lit table, and vast. Sounds from without the village indicated that various nocturnal animals had wakened. Jane giggled nervously, and Morton ostentatiously yawned.

Magnuson looked at Jones. "I told you that more than our individuals lives is here at stake. We find ourselves privileged to aid the forces that on another world created us. To become evolution's conscious and willing tools. The Kappan hominid is on the verge of becoming human, and chance has given us the opportunity to help."

Red Circles had been leaning on his spear, a few paces from the table. Now he stirred restlessly.

Magnuson looked over at him, as if accepting a challenge implied by the movement. "What are the Forest People, Red Circles? Are they men?"

"They are enemies or slaves, Magnuson."

"But, when some of them have become men, full men like you and me, what then?"

"Magnuson you know they are our enemies. I have

seen you torture them, and it was good. Now these others from Earth will help us kill the grown Forest People and make the young ones our slaves. And we will hide all of you, when your enemies come flying to find you. All this will be good too."

Magnuson sighed with weary impatience. "Red Circles, I do not mean to kill the Forest People or to make them slaves, and well you know it. You have learned new speech from me, with great skill; can you not learn more than speech? When the Forest People have become full men, like you and me, then it will be wrong to kill them, or to keep them at work by whipping."

"Yes," said Red Circles. "When they are men." He was not arguing with Magnuson, but neither was he giving way.

Magnuson looked round the table at his fellow Earth-descended. "How many men and women, do you think, upon how many worlds, have lived out the lives of baboons, among families of less-than-man? How many bearing within them the spark of humanity have spent their days and years grubbing for insects, beside their animal parents and siblings? I tell you, it is happening here and now, on Kappa.

"Tomorrow, we are all going up the river to the Workers' Village. The council of chiefs has decided that a new temple is to be built, and the stone quarry up there is busy. You will see how the hominids are used in the quarry. They are beasts of burden, but among those beasts I fear that there are slaves."

"Helping the poor slaves is all very fine," said Pete Kaleta, wiping grease from his hands. "But you know what we want."

"I sent you some of the Water of Thought,"
Magnuson replied stiffly. "In payment for the radio
and the other things you got for me. And for your
silence. As if you didn't want silence for yourselves."

"Yes, you gave us a little of the stuff. But just a
sample. Well, the people in the Outfit want some
more. They like something with a real kick to it, I
understand. Don't look so disgusted. You knew who
we were doing business with. Now I swear to you,
Magnuson, I mean to deliver the stuff we've
contracted for." Kaleta looked round; Red Circles
had walked away, and no other Kappan was listening, but he lowered his voice anyway. "That's going
to take a lot of Thought-Water, and it's going to
mean a lot of money. A lot. We'll give you a share of
the profits. You can spend it doing things for these
hominids, if that's what you live for. But understand, you're going to help us make the delivery."

Magnuson looked at Kaleta and Morton as if they
were filth just dropped onto his supper table. Then
he turned to Jones and Boris. "Gentlemen, as you
know, I have quarreled with the Space Force. Daily I
violate its narrow-minded rules restricting anthro-
pological research, but I still respect it and I respect
you. When I see such as these . . . . "

"Don't get tough." Morton's voice was icy. Then
he smiled over at Jones. "I understand you're going
to make a good customer for the Water from now
on. Stick with us and we'll see that you're taken care
of."

Jones stared back. Then he put his face down in
his hands on the table.

In the small hut where he and Boris were quartered for the night, Jones poured himself a sip of the Water of Thought. Then he sat on a stool silently clutching his stone bottle, which appeared to be nearly empty.

"You look sick," said Boris, rocking on his own stool. They had been allowed a small oil lamp, but no table to put it on, so it burned on the dirt floor.

"I am sick. Feverish. Magnuson hasn't given me any more of the stuff yet. It may be killing me, but I don't mind if it does. If only I wouldn't imagine strange things. That's the part that gets me." Jones got up, went to the open doorway of the hut and looked out. Then he came back and stretched out on a sleeping mat. He had recapped his bottle and he still held it tightly.

"What sort of things?"

Jones did not answer. After a while he seemed to sleep.

Boris went to the doorway and sat down there cross-legged, looking out at the fire-spotted village night. He wondered where the groundsuits and the rifles were being kept. Not that the knowledge would do him much good if he had it. Against a tree in the middle distance there leaned a warrior with a spear, visible in silhouette, probably watching Boris.

Kaleta and Morton had not seemed to be worried about the Space Force. Doubtless the cruiser was late, and doubtless before it got here the smugglers planned to have a barrel of Thought-Water stowed away, and no inconvenient witnesses on hand.

The rest of the colonists were probably staying

close to their firesides on the mayor's advice, and thinking with admiration of heroic Mayor Kaleta, brave Don Morton, and fearless Jane whatever-her-name-was, who were all out risking their necks in the wilderness to rescue Brenda and Boris from the berserk killer Jones . . . .

On the other side of the village common, a slender figure had just appeared beside a small fire. It was Jane, and she was looking about her as if in search of someone or something.

Boris found himself free to stand up and walk out of the hut. Jane watched his approach, and smiled tentatively when he drew near.

"How goes the plotting?" Boris asked, moving up beside her. Though the night was not cold, he spread his hands out toward the fire. It seemed an ancient, almost instinctive gesture.

"Not too well, I think." Jane's voice was like her body, small, firm, and quick. Her hair was lighter than Brenda's, her face thinner, to Boris less suggestive of sensuality. "Don and the good mayor have walked back to the copter; they're going to radio back to the colony that all's well with them and me but we haven't found you or Brenda yet. I suppose you're worried about Brenda?"

"Sure, not to mention myself. But how about you?"

"What do you mean, how about me?"

"I mean should I be worrying over what might be done to you—or what you might do?"

Jane gave her nervous laugh. "Both, I guess. I admit I'd like to be rich, and I'd like to get off this planet permanently with Don. Or someone, not Don if I can help it. But I really don't want to hurt anyone in the process. And I don't want to get arrested. Isn't that a laugh?"

"No."

"No." Jane's eyes became sympathetic. "Boris, what's happened to you? I can see something's—wrong."

"I drank the Water of Thought. I lost my—free will." Boris's voice cracked, and he realized that he was suddenly very close to breaking down. He had lost count of the hours and days of his helplessness. "I have to follow Jones's orders. If he told me to stick my head into this fire, do it."

"Don't say that!" Jane cried, quietly, impulsively. Her sympathy was undoubtedly sincere. She took a step toward Boris, and gripped his arm as if to save him from the flames.

Having her do that was more help than he would have believed. "I'll be all right," he said in a moment, and put his big hand over hers. "Are you involved in this dope-peddling? Not yet, eh?"

"No. Not yet." Jane let go of him, and shivered. Now it was her turn to spread her hands to the fire as if for warmth. "But I'm afraid of Don. Why haven't you asked about Brenda?"

"How is she?" He had judged it wiser not to show concern.

"All right, except for her sore ankle. Magnuson treated that for her. She's sleeping now. Boris, you don't think I'm ugly, do you?"

"Not by Earth-descended standards, certainly. Under normal conditions I might well be chasing you around the fire."

"No, you'd be chasing Brenda. Oh, I'm her friend, really, Boris, but I do have this streak of . . . envy. Whenever she has someone or something that I don't have, I envy her. Maybe that's how I got started with Don. He was after her, though she was too smart to ever be much interested in him."

"What kind of a guy is Morton?"

"Not very nice. He can be mean, very mean, Boris. I've been around him enough to know."

"And you never guessed what he and Kaleta were up to?"

"That's fairly recent. I knew something was going on. I was hoping it was something that would make enough money for Don to take me offworld with him. I guess I was afraid to find out what it really was, but I didn't think it'd be anything this bad!"

"But you knew it was connected somehow with Magnuson?"

"I found out little bits of things, here and there. Dr. Magnuson made himself vanish, out here in the hills. Then he sent a Kappan he trusted to Don at the colony, telling Don there was something up that might make a lot of money. Oh, he knew what Donnie boy is like, all right. And the mayor, too. Magnuson scares me."

"What kind of help did Magnuson want?"

"Oh, radio equipment, so he could listen in and tell if anyone was searching for him. Other things, some scientific equipment, I don't know. You ask a lot of questions."

"It's about all I can do."

"Oh, Boris, I wish it wasn't so. And to handle everything Don had to cut the mayor in. Mayor

Pete's greedy, too. Even greedier than Don, I guess."

"So they're using Magnuson and he's using them. Interesting. Any one else in on it?"

"No. Oh, you mean Brenda?" Jane gave him a cold, bright smile, and shook her head almost regretfully. "No. I'm good at keeping secrets."

Boris returned the smile. "So, here we are. You still think you might get rich, and get away from this planet, and not have dope-smuggling and maybe murder on your conscience when you do. But really you know that the Space Force is almost sure to uncover all this sooner or later, because so many people are involved." Boris himself was not so sure as he made himself sound. "And when that time comes, you'd like to have me as your friend. If I'm still alive."

Jane put her hand on his arm again. "I'll do what I can for you, Boris. Yes, for Brenda too. But I can't do much." She raised the hand and traced with one finger the line of his jaw. "You know, I could wish you were under *my* control, not Eddie's. But Don will be coming back. I'd better go."

Boris was almost back at the doorway of his hut when he realized that a man was standing motionless in the shadows beside it. It was Magnuson.

When Boris stopped, the doctor took a step forward, cleared his throat, and said self-consciously: "I order you to stand on your head."

"What?" Boris felt an almost hysterical urge to giggle. Then he understood. "Oh, a test. No, Doctor, I don't have to obey your orders. Only Jones's."

"Good. Then you will not obey Morton or Kaleta either. Will you step into the hut?"

Inside, three warriors held Jones. His arms were bound, and there was a flint knife at his throat.

"Jones controls you. And now, as you see, I control Jones." Magnuson was not boasting; he was miserable. "Oh, this is all horrible. But I must remain in control, and there is no other way to do it."

Jones spoke without moving his head. "Brazil, he wants you to get into a groundsuit and disarm Morton and Kaleta. Wait until they finish with the radio and come back to the village. It shouldn't be too hard a job."

Boris looked from Jones to Magnuson. "You don't need to compel me to do that—just give me permission."

"I hate to use you as a slave." Magnusom was suffering. "But I have done worse things. Yes.

"I know you'd escape in a moment if you could. Perhaps you'd kill me, and that would end my work. So I must control you in the groundsuit and get you out of it again. I hope that I can soon convince you that what I do here is the work of Man. But in the meantime—"

There came a muffled clanking at the doorway of the hut. Red Circles and two others bore a groundsuit in.

Jones gave precise orders. "Brazil, put the groundsuit on. Disarm Kaleta and Morton, but don't hurt them if you can help it. Then come at once back to this hut and take off the suit." He glanced at Magnuson, who nodded. The flint knife was eased a few centimeters away from Jones's throat.

"I think I will be the one to take the weapons from the two Earthmen," Red Circles said.

"No." Magnuson looked steadily at the war chief. "They will be on their guard, and you might have to kill them, especially if you went alone against them."

Muscles bunched along Red Circles' jaw. "Magnuson does not say that I might fail."

"I know you better than that. But bad as they are, I do not want the two Earthmen killed. I mean to provide them with a chance to prove themselves true men."

Red Circles appeared to understand, if not to agree.

Magnuson stared off briefly into space, fascinated by something that only he could see. "Like a baptism," he mused. "It may wash away past sins."

Boris, getting into the suit, thought that he understood. Magnuson had said earlier that all of the Earthmen present would become members of this tribe. Then the "baptism" would be an initiation ceremony.

"There may be shooting," Boris said to Magnuson. "Better see that the village people keep their heads down."

"Yes, that's right." Magnuson hurried out of the hut.

"One thing," said Boris to Jones.

"What?" Jones opened his eyes. He had seemed to be resting on his stool, almost oblivious to the Kappans who stood by ready to kill him at a moment's notice.

"Let me make sure that Brenda's safe."

Jones sighed. "I'll ask them to bring her over here so you can see she's healthy—as soon as you come back here and get out of that suit."

And that had to suffice. Boris went out of the hut, wrapped now in the familiar fluid power of a groundsuit, but as helpless as ever. Outside, he met Magnuson and strode across the village common with him.

"They'll come back to the village along that path," Magnusom whispered to him, pointing in the starlight. "The copter is in a clearing over there. Remember, no bloodshed."

"I want none."

"Of course. Good luck." Magnuson moved silently away.

I don't need luck now, thought Boris, watching the greater darkness of the path where it emerged from the forest. Later he would need all the luck available, when he tried to resist his orders, when he attempted to keep the suit on and pick up Brenda and carry her away to safety.

A flashlight appeared, far down the path. Moving expertly in the bulky suit, Boris took shelter behind some bushes. He turned up the sensitivity of his helmet's microphones, and picked up a low murmur of voices.

"—anything fatal to Brenda, at least not right away. That'd be a terrible waste," Don Morton chuckled.

"Let's get the *business* settled." Kaleta sounded angry. "We'll be lucky to manage that, without playing around."

"All right, all right. Anyone who's dead or missing can be blamed on Jones afterwards. I suppose eventually there's bound to be some kind of investigation."

"So we want to get the Kappans on our side. And we play along with Magnuson until we find out where the stuff comes from."

They were very close to Boris now, and evidently Kaleta caught the gleam of his suit through the bushes. He stopped, grabbing at Morton; the flashlight in Morton's hand swung suddenly to shine into the thicket.

"Who?" demanded Kaleta sharply.

"Me," said Boris, and plunged after Morton, who had spun around and was dashing back along the path toward the copter. The race was no contest. Morton heard the metal footfalls closing in, turned, and fired. Bullets whanged off the armored suit before Boris got a grip on the barrel of the machine pistol, yanked it from Morton's grasp, and bent it into uselessness.

"Come along." With compelled gentleness, Boris took Morton's arm and towed him back toward the village. Morton made choking sounds of rage and fear, but offered no more resistance.

The good mayor had been smart enough to raise his hands and stand still. Boris plucked Kaleta's firearm from its holster and squeezed it into junk. Then, gripping one man's arm lightly in each metal gauntlet, Boris marched his prisoners back into the village and across the common.

Magnuson met them, an escort of warriors at his back. His face showed relief. Jane and Brenda stood

JANET AULISIO © 1980

beside him.

"I'm all right, Boris," Brenda called to him. There was hope in her eyes again.

Nothing would be easier now than to rage through them all, knocking them aside until he had Brenda safe in his metal arms; then, to run with her, spears bouncing from his back, trees crashing under his feet, carrying her safe through the night toward the sheltering forcefield walls of the colony.

Boris removed his helmet, then his suit. He could not even try to disobey.

V.

In the morning, again transmitting his orders through Jones, Magnuson had Boris once more put on a groundsuit, then drag the other suit to the river and throw it into a deep pool, together with the energy rifles.

"We are going upstream," Magnuson announced, when the rest of his prisoners had been assembled to hear him. "A few kilometers north of here at the Workers' Village there are some things that I want all of you to see. Probably we will stay at the Workers' Village tonight, and tomorrow go on upstream again. Farther that way lies the Warriors' Village. There, in a day or two, we shall all of us learn whether we are acceptable to the Spirit of Man."

"You're out of your head," Morton told him.

"I know you think so, now. But come."

When the march upstream was organized, Magnuson led the way, with Red Circles and an elaborately robbed chief priest at his sides. Boris, still wearing the groundsuit, followed, accompanied by Brenda and Jane. Then Kaleta and Morton, both sullenly silent. After a few more priests, a small

JANET AULISIO ©1980

band of warriors brought up the rear, with Jones secured among them, gagged so he could shout no sudden orders to Boris.

The path between villages was a well-worn trail, but steep in places and fairly difficult. It zig-zagged uphill among boulders and under overshadowing trees. Brenda was still limping, though Magnuson had treated her ankle. Boris helped her over the rougher spots. He found that he was hardly able to speak to her. Her eyes were sympathetic and not accusing—but still it was harder and harder for him to meet them with his own.

After the first kilometer and a half the trail climbed beside a low waterfall and then smoothed out. Now it wound along beside the Yunoee through cultivated fields in a broad, flat valley. Trees were widely scattered here; anyone scouting in a copter could easily have seen the procession, spotted the Earth-descended people and the glinting groundsuit. Magnuson kept looking up and around at the sky, but it was empty of machines.

A few kilted fields hands looked up, from their labor or rest, to gape at the procession as it passed. Soon another cluster of small buildings came into view ahead.

The Workers' Village, like the Temple Village, straddled the narrow Yunoee. But instead of a temple this settlement was centered on sheds, where logs and stone were worked and stored. A kilted worker-chief came forth to greet Magnuson and the other two chiefs as equals. The six captive Earth-descended people caused much curiosity, almost all of it polite, among the workers.

Again Boris was ordered out of the groundsuit, and it was carried away to some hiding place; then Jones could be relieved of his gag. After that Magnuson's prisoners were only casually watched.

After talking privately until mid-day with the other chiefs, Magnuson came to share a meal with the six other Earth-descended. He ate quickly and sparingly, as usual, then rose to speak.

"I have persuaded the other chiefs to begin the annual rite of passage tomorrow night. When this year's class of young Kappans face their test, we all of us will go with them." He smiled happily at the two young women. "You of course will go to the women's ceremony, somewhat earlier. Things will be much easier for you than they will for us."

Kaleta jumped to his feet. "What are you getting us into?"

Magnuson smiled at him briefly. "Why, Mr. Mayor, I am giving you a chance."

"To enter a tribe of savages?"

"One who promotes organized crime has no right to use that word of others. It is true, that if you survive, you will find the tribal secrets open to you, and these warriors sworn to defend you like a brother. But what I am talking about is a greater chance that that. If you can prove your own humanity and your own manhood, to yourself, I think you will care less for peddling dope."

"And if I can't—prove myself, as you put it—to you?"

"Not to me, Mr. Mayor. To yourself, and to the tribe. I'll be beside you, undergoing the same things. And if we fail? Why, then we will die—deservedly."

Kaleta sat down, as if his legs were suddenly too weak to hold him; his plump face had turned grayish. Morton sat beside him, smoldering. Boris, watching, derived a certain satisfaction from the look of the two smart operators as they revised their opinion of the crackpot who wanted to be a savage and could somehow be disposed of easily when the time was ripe.

Magnuson turned from the table. "Come along, all of you. This afternoon I want to show you something of my work."

He led them west from the Workers' Village, at right angles to the river's course. The path here was wide and dusty, scarred as if by the frequent dragging of heavy objects. When they had gone a few hundred meters, staccato shouting and the cracking of whips could be heard from a short distance ahead, behind a screen of trees.

The path, emerging from the forest, spread to form a broad grassless area rimming a quarry pit. Over the wide pit dust hung in the air. Along its edge kilted workers were shaping blocks of stone with saws of copper or bronze, the first metal tools that Boris had seen in native Kappan hands.

But stonecutting and metal tools were not what Magnuson had in mind to show them. "There," he said, and pointed.

Up over the lip of the quarry-pit, moving with painful slowness through a haze of dust, beasts of burden came into view. They appeared a pair at a time, gripping a crude rope with their human hands, hauling upward with all their strength. There were eight of the short, two-legged beasts in the team, and they dragged uphill a sledge weighted with a single stone block. Under the flicking whip of a kilted overseer, the hominids moved their load without outcry. Their naked leathery skins were white with the dry dust of the quarry. One of the two females in the team was obviously pregnant.

Magnuson gestured for his little group of sightseers to accompany him as he moved forward to the rim of the pit. Now Boris could see down into the quarry, where other groups of hominids were toiling. He had seen slaves before; he had seen humanity in most of its known themes abused and brutalized upon a score of planets. The sight before him now was somehow different from anything that he had seen before, and he could not decide at once if it was worse or not as bad. These hominid faces, prime theme though they were, outwardly resembling *homo sapiens,* showed nothing Boris could identify as human hope or hate, fear or resentment. Their five-fingered hands expressed nothing, hung limp when not gripping rope or pushing stone. None of the beasts had been given work requiring tools. The kilted men with whips barked out their orders in repeated monosyllables, as if to horses.

If these beasts were the product of some brainwasher's art, then the most accomplished tyrants of the Galaxy might be able to learn new skills on Kappa. But no, thought Boris. These two-legged brutes have never been human.

Jane had turned away from the sight. But Brenda watched, and Boris saw tears in her eyes.

"It is not as simple as it seems," said Magnuson to her gently. "If they had the bodies of horses, and you saw them given food and water and rest, you would not weep for them. They are given those things."

"But they're not horses," objected Brenda.

"Ah, that's the point, yes. Weep for those who are not. Perhaps as many as one in five, even one in three, must bear in their brains the spark of humanity. And that spark has never been fanned."

"Why do you say they must?" Kaleta asked.

"Look at them. Think about them. They can hardly be anywhere else on the evolutionary tree. In the wild state they are quite capable of using weapons, to fight the villagers and no doubt in hunting also. Biology is not really my field, but their cranial capacity seems quite adequate for abstract thought. It's true that apes will now and then use tools. But the ape brain is always smaller, and the forelimbs adapted primarily for travel, whether brachiating or walking. In the prime theme tree only man and his immediate ancestors habitually stand erect. Come this way. I'll show you my laboratory."

Magnuson led them away from the quarry, along a narrow, little-used path that curved through the woods for a hundred meters and ended at a big, new-looking cabin of solid log construction. At one end of this building was a pen of upright logs, like a prison stockade.

Inside the stockade were eight hominids. The one female and one of the males looked old and completely crippled, obviously unable to to any longer haul stone in the quarry. The remaining six were all younger males, all comparatively healthy-

looking, though one of them was minus a hand.
Looking more carefully at the six, Boris saw that
each bore the scar of some serious but now healed
injury. Probably primitive ropes broke often in the
quarry, and heavy stones slipped and slid and fell.

A water trough ran into the pen. "Dry again,"
sighed Magnuson, taking up a pail. He began to fill
the trough up from a nearby well. "I can't get the
villagers to feed or water a hominid that does no
work. They give me the ones that are badly injured
in quarry accidents, and my first aid and Earth
drugs save some of them, as you see. Red Circles will
not understand that my treatments are not meant as
torture. There, you were all thirsty, weren't you?"

Inside the pen, the hominids had clustered along
the trough, cupping up water in their hands, or
bending over to slurp noisily. The one-handed male
drank, then turned and reached out between the
logs of the palisade toward Magnuson. Magnuson
touched the gray leathery hand, as if knowing that
was all the creature wanted.

"Have they any speech?" Jones asked. He was
staring with an odd expression at the hominids.

"No. Oh, according to the villagers, the wild
adults have a language of their own. But I doubt it's
more than a system of warning cries such as monkeys
use. I've never been close enough to a wild adult to
hear it myself."

"But they must have a speech. I can remember —"
Jones abruptly stopped speaking. He stared at the
hominids as if something about them frightened
them. They were paying him no attention.

Magnuson shook his head, watching Jones carefully. "No, they have no speech. The young ones are captured when they wander away from the wild troop, then brought here and trained like horses or dogs. I've tried to teach them to speak a few words, but I think none of them is psychically ready for symbolic thought. So I mean for the six young males here to go with us tomorrow night, into the rite of passage."

Boris, having followed Magnuson's thought this far, was not surprised. He tried to picture members of three species being initiated into the same tribe— he didn't yet know the details of the initiation, but he could imagine what it would be like. Still, he refrained for the time being from arguing.

Jones was surprised. He asked: "Will the villagers stand for it?"

Magnuson nodded. "Just barely. Oh, perhaps all six of these will die in the ordeal, for no mere animal can pass through alive. But in pain and shock is man born, as an individual or as a race. If the ordeal awakens none of these six to manhood, why I must try again; I must somehow get time to try again. In the end I must succeed. Then I shall have made man, and what our so-called civilization does to me will not matter."

Morton, who had been silently expressing disdain, now laughed. "You'll play hell starting a tribe with those. Six males."

Magnuson was unruffled. "The female is not so important." He bowed, smiling, to the two young women in the tour. "Until civilization is attained. And even then a psychic difference remains, which we ignore to our cost. What we now call civilization

abandons the formal rite of passage, and thereby
enfeebles the race. Eventually we must return on our
home planets to the ordeal to the weeding-out. Only
males who can prove their manhood should survive
long enough to reproduce."

Magnuson's Earth-descended audience heard him
in silence, angry, fearful, or indifferent. Maybe,
thought Boris, some of them half believed him. But
Magnuson was not interested right now in their reac-
tions. The one-armed hominid still stood at the
palisade, thrusting out both hand and stump
between the logs. Magnuson touched the gray hand
again.

After feeding his hominids, throwing leaves and
roots from a bin into the pen, he beckoned again to
his visitors. "Come inside, all of you."

Most of the interior of the large cabin was a single
room, floored with stone slabs. There were village-
made worktables and shelves, holding a scattering of
books and papers, a small computer, various
chemical and electrical apparatus.

"I took a chance, stealing this for you," said
Kaleta, pointing to a microscope under a dusty
plastic cover. "Why'd you want it, if you're not
working with the Water of Thought?"

"I was mainly interested in the Water, at first.
Drinking it, as I have mentioned, brought me here.
But once here I turned to more important things.
Yes. I've now almost entirely given over the physical
and chemical sides of research. But here, here's an
interesting bit of physical evidence."

From a table Magnuson picked up a skull of somewhat less than adult Earthman size but still, thought

Boris, of a brain capacity probably sufficient for intelligence. It was certainly prime theme shape. The teeth were omnivorous, human-looking, and noticeably worn — probably a quarry-beast chewed a lot of grit along with its rough food. The jaw was short, heavy, almost chinless. Below a receding forehead the supraorbital ridges stood out boldly, joining together between the eyes.

"What do you think about it, gentlemen?" Magnuson spoke to Jones and Boris.

Jones, briefly a planeteer again, accepted the skull. He turned it in his hands, looking at the face, the sides, and the top of the cranium. "Prime theme presapient hominid. Rare, but hardly astonishing."

"Correct. Now, tell me, upon how many planets has the transition from beast to human been observed? The achievement of sapience, in any theme, prime or otherwise?"

Jones shrugged. "It's never been observed, as far as I know, but that's not surprising. If you want to talk technical evolutionary theory, it's an instance of the automatic suppression of a peduncle. The beginnings of anything tend to be out of sight and out of reach."

"Right again." Magnuson nodded, smiling and intent. "But here and now, upon this world, the rare moment is before us. Or it will be, if we choose to create it. And I so choose."

Jones put down the skull, and leaned wearily against the table. "All this has ceased to concern me, or I'd argue with your methods."

"Argue, then. I've told you that your slavery to the Water of Thought will probably soon be over."

"If I'm soon dead, it will." Jones displayed a sickly smile. "If I argue with you, will that induce you to refill my bottle?"

"No. But I can promise you that you'll drink the Water of Thought at least once more. We all will, on beginning the initiation ceremony."

Kaleta and Morton almost jumped at Magnuson, cursing him and demanding explanations; Boris came near joining them.

"I tried to have you all exempted from drinking," Magnuson said. "But the chiefs refused. They gave in to me on the more important point of letting the hominids participate, so I would not press them on this."

Only Jones relaxed. "Then I won't argue. I'll accept as true any theory that brings me more of the Water."

"If you won't argue," Boris said, "I will. Our going through a paddling to join some half-wit fraternity is not going to prove anything, except that we'd rather suffer than die. Neither will it prove much about your hominid pupils here, as far as I can see. If you can't educate them now, a torture session won't make them any smarter. What's wrong with just letting them along, to go to hell in their own way? That's all the Space Force wants, as I see it. And for once I tend to agree with my bosses."

But it was no use; he was not getting through to Magnuson. They were thinking in different co-ordinate systems. Well, Boris had expected argument to fail, but he had had to try.

Magnuson faced Boris more in sadness than in anger. Or perhaps he was controlling his anger well.

"Oh, yes. I am — what is the phrase? — a do-gooder. I interfere. My interference in evolutionary processes has been forbidden, on this and other planets. I remember the words of one Tribune — she said my work would be cruel, cruel to animals and humans both. As if hominids and humans alike were not already on the anvil of evolution! The only mercy granted the Kappan hominids now is their ignorance of the transformation that lies just beyond their reach. Cruel! Perhaps that Tribune would forbid a woman to give birth, because the experience would be likely to traumatize her child."

"Well, I can't stop you." Boris picked up the hominid skull from the table, and on a hunch turned it upside down. The *foramen magnum* had been enlarged by crude hacking into a gaping hole, big enough to have permitted extraction of the brain.

Magnuson was smiling at Boris's discovery. "Yes, more evidence of proto-humanity. When one of the hominids dies in the quarry, the others usually cut or break open the skull, and devour at least part of the brain. Unpleasant, yes. But still, as a twentieth-century anthropologist wrote: 'Nearly the most ancient human trick we know.'"

Boris sat on a log at one side of the sunny common of the Workers' Village, while Brenda stood behind him, massaging his tired neck. Children, kilted and kiltless, goggled shyly and laughed at them.

"How's your ankle now?" he asked.

"Not bad. Better than it was. Afraid I wouldn't get far, though, if I tried to run for help."

"I can't do that, or anything," he said. "I've tried."

"I know you have. You'll get over it, though. You will."

"Magnuson thinks that Jones and I will recover in another day or two. I suppose just in time to drink more of the stuff for the ceremony. But Magnuson isn't trusting me in the groundsuit any more."

"That's a good sign. Isn't it?"

"I suppose it is. But I can't afford to start hoping." That was a shameful thing to say, especially to anyone as brave as Brenda was turning out to be. But Boris said it. He could feel himself hitting bottom.

Quartered that night with Jones in a hut in the Workers' Village, Boris dreamed again. He was a hominid, dragging a heavy sledge up the side of a quarry-pit. He felt a whip. Planeteer Hayashi was behind him, pulling desperately with one hand at the monstrous growth upon his face, and lashing Boris with the other.

VI.

In the morning the Earth-descended were served a breakfast of fruit, stewed meat, and freshly baked bread. A pair of robed priests arrived from the lower village, and helped Magnuson lead his six young hominids from their pen, after first roping them together like hand-bound mountaineers. Then the procession of the day before, enlarged now by hominids and more priests, moved on upstream. This time the groundsuit was left behind, and Jones was no longer so closely guarded.

After a couple of kilometers the flat valley pinched in again, becoming a gorge through which the Yunoee tumbled. Again the trail became difficult; but the group moved at an unhurried pace, and the journey was short.

The Warriors' Village at the influx of a tributary creek, straddled the Yunoee as had the two settlements below. In this settlement the huts were roughly made, and crudely shingled with thorny bark.

Here the villagers' greeting was a screaming mob scene. Boris put his arms protectively round both Jane and Brenda as howling warriors leaped past

them, brandishing knives and clubs. But the Earth-descended were not really menaced. It was the roped-together hominids that drew the brunt of the threatening uproar. It took all the shouting and gesturing that Magnuson and the robed witch-men could manage to keep the hominids from being physically assailed and probably slaughtered. The hominids cowered and snarled, huddling together inside a ring of screaming warriors and squaws. Magnuson needed half an hour to get his pupils into the village, to the comparative safety of a pen that had been built for them.

Boris had little worry to spare for hominids. He was relieved when the village women took gentle custody of Brenda and Jane and led them away, evidently to some ceremony which males were forbidden to attend.

While Magnuson conferred with the chiefs, the four other Earthmen were shown where they were to stay. Kaleta and Morton sat down and whispered together. Jones paced restlessly around the portion of the village where he was allowed to go. Boris sat down in the abandoned hut in which he and Jones had been billeted, and tried to keep out of trouble.

He had been there only a few minutes when a shadow darkened the green brightness of the doorway, and Morton stepped in.

"Brazil, you're still under Jones's orders, huh?"

"Yes. But I can defend myself if need be."

"I didn't come in to start a fight." Morton seated himself on the dirt floor. "Look, do you know anything about this initiation business Magnuson's got us into?"

"Not this one in particular. I've seen 'em on other

planets."

"What's the best way to get through one?"

"You're asking me for help? When do you plan to murder me?"

"All right, so I've got a lot of nerve. I said I didn't come in here for trouble, but you don't scare me a damn bit, colonel, or whatever the hell you are. You don't have your tin suit on now."

Jones came in. "What's this all about?"

Morton stood up. "Maybe *you'll* tell me something about this initiation thing. After it's all over you're going to want me around to fill your bottle for you."

Jones's cheek started twitching. "There's no big secret about getting through an initiation. As Brazil says, it's not much different from joining some half-wit fraternity. Just grit your teeth and follow orders, and don't try to fight back."

Morton nodded slowly. "That's about what I thought. And it might get pretty rough, right? Suppose we tried to get out of here, today or tonight, what do you think our chances would be?"

"Just about zero," said Jones, "and I don't want to get away."

"That's right, you'll do anything to stay near the Thought-Water." Morton thought for a moment. "Well, I agree with you, for once. I've gone through a lot already to get my hands on that stuff. I'm not about to give up now."

When Morton had gone out, Jones sat down, his cheek still twitching. He pulled his little stone bottle out of a coverall pocket. "Brazil, you're lucky. If and when you're cured, you're a free man. If I'm cured of this I'm still a murderer."

"Temporary insanity might be a good defense."

"Legally, I suppose. But I'll still know what I've done, and why, and how it felt to give up everything for this. For water. You know if I lose the Water now, I won't have anything."

"You think we'll be cured, Jones?"

"Magnuson thinks so. And he's so calmly sure of everything it's hard to argue with him. Right now he's debating with the chiefs again. They still don't like the idea of initiating his six hominids, but he's still insisting, and he'll probably win. He's quite a man."

"He is. But what chance will his hominids have in an initiation?"

"Almost none. They don't know what it's all about, ritual, ties of blood, sacrifice. They're just simple, ignorant people."

"People?"

Jones raised the dry bottle to his mouth, holding it vertical to drain any last possible drop. Then he hurled it across the hut, and began to laugh, in quiet near-hysteria.

"They're people," Jones said. "I'm mad, but I know. Don't ask me how." With that he collapsed, laughing or sobbing.

Boris sat quietly, looking out into the green Kappan sunshine.

Somehow, the day passed, and most of the night.

In the dark pre-dawn Boris found himself suddenly awake, listening to a distant rumble of drums, and to a howl like that of whirled bull-roarers. Across the hut, Jones too was awake, and sitting up. Before either could speak, the hut was filled with warriors, masked and painted as Boris had never seen them before. He was jerked to his feet and dragged from the hut with Jones beside him. Their escort was joined by another little swarm of warriors surrounding Morton and Kaleta, and the whole mob moved out of the village, taking by torchlight the path that climbed yet farther upstream beside the riverbank. Magnuson was ahead of them on the path, going in the same direction under his own power, holding the lead end of a rope which the six cowering hominids gripped like blind men traversing a place of danger.

There was much howling and jostling. Boris staggered and scrambled and was pushed along. Torchlight fell on frenzied or frightened faces, on night-black river water and the white curl of rapids. Ahead the sky was lit by a huge fire, and from there came the sounds of drum and bull-roarer.

The steep riverbanks fell away again as the place of the fire drew near. The procession moved on into the glare and the heat of the flames before it halted. The young villagers who were candidates for initiation were standing beside the fire already, in kilt or robe or loincloth, frightened but trying to be stoic. The five Earthmen and the six hominids were pushed in among their group. The drums were very loud.

"Tell Brazil that he is free," Magnuson shouted to Jones. "Until he has passed through the ordeal, or failed it, he must act for himself. Tell him!"

"All right." Jones turned to Boris. "So be it. You're on your own, sink or swim."

Boris hated both of them. He was not property, not a robot to be turned off or on. And at the moment, any talk of his having freedom was a bad joke. The hands of half a dozen warriors were on him, pulling off his clothes. Each candidate for tribal membership was first stripped, then draped with a net-like garment of tough fibers, weighted with fist-sized stoned. Someone thrust another such rock, painted with a crude design, into Boris's hand, making sure that his fingers gripped it tightly.

"Hold on to your rock at all costs," Magnuson was shouting at the other Earthmen. "To drop it means to reject the use of tools, and if you drop it you will be killed."

The candidates were pushed into a ring, scorchingly close to the fire. A warrior thrust a cup under Boris's nose; he drank, draining the vessel, and the Water of Thought was cool and familiar in his throat. Beside him, Jones gasped, and drank; they had to tear the empty cup away from him. The hominids gulped, like so many thirsty animals. The young villagers, tasting the drug for the first time, swallowed it with reverence. Boris could not see how Magnuson and Kaleta and Morton faced the moment; they were now somewhere on the other side of the fire from him.

Someone screamed a signal and a dance began, the candidates circling the fire, the warriors keeping pace with them in an outer ring, flourishing weapons and leaping in the firelight, to the roar of drums.

Boris, positioned in the inner ring between a village youth and one of the hominids, jigged and hopped, doing what seemed to be expected of him. Somehow the hominids were moving with the others, so far at least, not dancing but keeping their relative places in the ring. What would the Water of Thought do to them? At least it had not paralyzed Boris again; he felt nothing from it yet.

One warrior leaped in from the outer circle, and slashed lightly with a small flint knife across the chest of one of the young villagers, who gave no sign of pain or shock. Then the man whirled back to his place in the outer ring, and others danced in, each to single out a different victim.

Boris felt a sudden sharp gouge on the back of one leg, and managed to keep himself from showing any reaction. The man who had wounded him now spun dancing past in front of Boris. He was masked, but Boris recognized Red Circles by his size and his painted arms. It was undoubtedly a compliment to be favored with the personal attention of the war chief, though not one that Boris could fully appreciate.

The creeping hypnosis of the drums and the dance was available, and Boris knew that it could help. He let himself move into it, gradually. He concentrated on holding a part of his mind ultimately clear, ready to take control.

Abruptly, screaming hell broke loose; the warriors had started to torment one of the hominids. Boris turned just in time to see the victim react with the simple directness of an animal, striking back with the sacred rock that it had been given to hold in its fist. In the next instant the hominid's body seemed to sprout spears like porcupine quills. Then it was only a gory and lifeless thing, being dragged away.

In the next moment, another hominid fought back, and died. And in the next, another. Between the explosions of violence only seconds elapsed, but Boris found himself able to think as if leisurely minutes were passing. The hypnotic influence of the dance had brought him to a state of observant detachment; he felt he was able to calculate long plans between throbs of the hammering drum. He saw the warriors with torture-knife and killing-spear, getting rid of their hominid enemies one after another, killing them within the rules of the ordeal, but with hair-trigger good will for the task. He saw Magnuson, standing still, arms half raised, ignoring his own fate, watching while his work and hope died on Kappan spear points.

And with this detached clarity, and tremendous speed of thought, Boris saw the fifth and sixth hominids still standing in their places behind Magnuson, while the fourth was dying before Magnuson's eyes.

Those remaining two hominids still stood, moving obediently with the circle, holding firmly to their ritual rocks, while one warrior jabbed at them with a point and another scorched them with a glowing stick. The two hominids watched Magnuson like dogs, and they obeyed him like trusting men, amid this violence and death. And Boris saw two warriors look at each other, look and come to silent agreement. They thrust with their spears, and the fifth hominid died, not by the rules of the passage, but by racist murder.

Then the two murderers saw Magnuson turn

toward them. And though he turned too late to see what they had done, they moved away as if ashamed, and so the sixth hominid still lived, under Magnuson's watchful eye.

To Boris all these things seemed to hold deep mystical significance. He knew that he was sliding deeper and still deeper into the hypnosis of rhythm and pain and the Water of Thought, and whatever else might be here at work; he knew it with the corner of his mind that was still normal, and had been assigned to hold control, but kept shrinking into less and less importance. Boris was not frightened now. Mayor Pete Kaleta hopped past him, glaring wildly, muttering his terror, but that meant nothing to Boris. Even Red Circles had become an unimportant figure, who now and then approached bringing unimportant torment.

That fifth hominid had died unjustly, killed by murderers who were false to the tribe and false to the spirit of man. Sometime Boris would tell the story, and see the murderers punished. Sometime in the future. But there was no future, really; this dance was eternal.

The figure of Magnuson drifted past, dancing mechanically, bending to look at the stained earth where his hominids had died, then looking up again, eyes prayerfully following the lone hominid survivor.

It was the young hominid with one hand.

Magnuson should be praying, now. There should be some atheists' prayer, to the Spirit of Man, that he could say.

Let us call you down, Man, from your abode of evolutionary law. Let our fire and the sound of our drum bring you descending through this planet's night to enter the brain's of those who dance for you. Make us all men. Make us all men. Boris could almost see the Spirit now, brooding in the rolling heat above the tongues of fire, coming and going with the heartbeat of the heaviest drum.

Then there was a disturbing noise that served to give his mind a foothold, and he fought his way up from deepening trance, pushing spirits and dreams away. One of the village adolescents had cracked and gone wild, had screamed and tried to run from the torture and the dance. And spearmen, ruthlessly obedient to the law of the ritual, forced their weapons home. The young Kappan died with a bubbling scream. Magnuson did not care about this one; Magnuson did not take his eyes from his hominid. But Boris saw the corpse dragged away. The sacred rock had fallen from the boy's hand, and a man kicked it into the fire.

Don Morton danced past; Boris was vaguely surprised to see him still alive. Morton's eyes were glazed, and he shouted incoherently. He did not blink when a warrior jabbed him.

The next thing Boris realized clearly was that the dance was over. The sun was touching the eastern horizon, and he and the other survivors were being led through the gloomy woods in torchlit silence. Was the ordeal finished? Not very likely.

Boris heard one awakening bird, and then found himself entering the mouth of a cave. His head still echoed with the now-silent drums, and his minor wounds blended into one pervasive ache, but it was not over yet. He was herded forward with the others,

into damp and stony silence.

The twisty passages of the cave linked together chambers so big that in some of them the torchlight died out without revealing all the walls. Feet shuffled behind Boris and ahead of him, along a well-worn trail, and from somewhere came the sound of trickling water. His throat burned with thirst, but he knew there was no use hoping for a drink.

The procession of candidates for manhood wound to a halt at last inside another enormous chamber. Here each candidate was made to sit in a separate niche among the rocks, isolated from sight of the others. Boris sat down with relief; there was a moment of rest and almost of peace.

Magnuson walked past him, croaking: "Do not move from where you have been placed, under pain of death. Do not move from where you have been placed—" He went on, repeating the warning, evidently for the other Earth-descended.

Sitting in his rocky niche, probably carved out many generations ago, Boris could see no one. In most directions, his field of view in the wavering, indirect torchlight extended hardly farther than his arm could reach. Directly behind him was a shadowy opening between rocks; it looked as if Something might crawl out of it at any moment. Directly in front of it was a sizable open space. Niches and folds of rock and stalagmites surrounded the open space like rows of seats around an arena; and now in the arena there gathered half a dozen robed medicine men, carrying torches and chanting.

As they sang, the witchmen began extinguishing their torches, one by one, so that the darkness grew up a leap at a time. Boris waited, fatalistically ready for whatever might come next. He was sitting tailor-fashion, holding his sacred rock on one knee, while the other stones tied to his net-garment dragged wearily down upon his shoulders.

Now only one torch still burned; the rocks of the cave all leaned and swayed with its light. The medicine men were close around it, doing something — Boris squinted through bleary eyes, and at last decided that they were lighting small shielded lanterns of some kind. And now the priest-chief, wearing the biggest mask and longest robe of all, had appeared in the arena. Another animal-skin robe, dripping wet, was in his hands. He raised the wet robe above his head, and slowly brought the night down with it, putting out the light. The last syllable of the chant died with the sputtering of the torch.

With sight gone, the sound of trickling water seemed louder. And now Boris was able to notice that the air in the cave was fresh, and that it was moving subtly past him. Probably there were several exits. A clever man might crawl silently through this darkness, find his way out, and be kilometers away in the woods, drinking safely from a fresh stream, before his tormentors even missed him. Never mind; any man who thought himself that clever would be certain to crawl into a trap and get himself speared to death. Still Boris could not free himself of the thought that escape was now a possibility. This cave seemed to have been designed for concealed movement.

At least, he told himself, he was now free to try. Or had his free will really been restored? Was Magnuson planning on the ordeal as part of the cure—

A hideous scream tore through the blackness, echoing and re-echoing, like some frenzied animal leaping from one wall to another of its cage. Boris kept himself under control. He continued to sit still. There was a shuffle of movement nearby and the sound of heavy breathing. The sounds died out again. Somewhere a Kappan boy began a hesitant, groping chant, as if inventing prayer.

Boris's eyes had slowly grown more sensitive in the darkness. Now he could detect a faint blur of light across the upper part of the cave.

"Brazil? Magnuson? Anyone near me?" The quiet voice was that of Jones, and it came from somewhere nearby on Boris's right.

No one jumped at Jones to kill him for speaking, so Boris judged it was probably safe to answer. "Brazil here. What's up?"

"Good. Listen, Brazil, some of these guys with the spears may have taken a drug to sharpen their night vision. Before this started I heard one of the women saying something about it."

"One of the women?" Talking was rough on the dried-out throat, but it might help the cause of sanity.

"Yes. Judging from what I heard, the women have their initiation in this cave too. None of them ever get killed; Brenda and Jane are probably having a feast with their new sisters right now. How long do you suppose we've been in here?"

"I don't know."

No one else seemed disposed to join the conversation. Either the other Earth-descended were out of earshot, or they thought that talking was too risky. Or they were simply saving their throats. There was silence for a little while.

"Brazil, you don't think I really wanted to leave my family, do you? Leave, abandon, everything I had and everything I was? Maybe you wanted to be a slave to this Water of Thought, but I didn't."

Boris's head jerked around. He stared into the darkness, toward the invisible Jones. "What do you mean, maybe I wanted to be a slave?"

"Well. Some people do want to get rid of all responsibility. It occurred to me."

For a moment Boris was unable to reply. He felt a great, hollow rage. *There's no truth at all in that*, he thought. *Not in my case. I wasn't tired of being responsible for myself.*

God. It couldn't be true, could it? He shivered, sitting still in the damp, moving air. It couldn't. But suppose . . .

Suppose that the effect of the Water of Thought upon an Earth-descended human, or human male at least, was this: to push the mind in whichever direction it happened to be leaning, making a fatal obsession out of what had been only a potential weakness.

Was this realization in itself the cure that Magnuson had predicted? Or was it the cure, but Magnuson didn't realize it?

From off among the rocks there came a sudden

weak flash of light—one of the dark lanterns flicked
open for just an instant. There was a startled gasp
from someone and then a return of darkness and
silence. After some timeless interval, another
lantern flashed in another part of the cave,
accompanied by sounds of sudden movement and a
cry of fear. Boris made his muscles relax and tried to
keep his mind on things other than thirst and
physical danger.

Perhaps it was well that he did, for the next light
that flashed illuminated the area just in front of
Boris, and he saw that between him and the lantern
crawled the figure of Red Circles, knife in hand. In
the next instant blackness had returned. Don't
move, Boris reminded himself, under penalty of
death. He would like to crack Red Circles on the
knuckles with a kilogram or so of sacred rock, that
would be more fun than moving even, but it too
might be considered bad form.

Surprise. Instead of the now-familiar pain of Red
Circles' dull knife, the lantern beam came again, in
the same place. Red Circles was not in sight. A
couple of meters in front of Boris on the cave floor,
just far enough so he would have to leave his place to
reach it, was a large cup holding something that
looked like water. The light went out again.

He was not to move from where they had placed
him; they would know, somehow, if he moved. But
Boris's memory held and enlarged the sight of that
cup, full to overflowing, a little water sloshed out
carelessly onto the stone floor as if the cup had just
been hastily set down. Boris's thirsty throat argued
that no one could notice a difference if a mouthful

of water were taken out. But his brain knew it was a trap. The cup might even be poisoned. If he had to, he could go a long time yet without drinking. And he had to.

He shifted and stretched his fingers, which were growing stiff from gripping the sacred tool-rock; it would not do to drop the thing by accident. Then he gave a little jump, and cursed, as Red Circles jabbed him nastily from behind, out of utter silence and darkness. Boris felt sure it had been Red Circles again; he thought that he could recognize the technique by now. He kept himself from trying to kill Red Circles.

What price free will now?

From somewhere in the cave there came an animal sound, a growling and snuffling that spoke plainly of a prowling predator. Boris's intellect insisted that it must be only a warrior doing imitations, and with some effort Boris kept his intellect firmly in control.

Soon, from close in front of him, came the faintest possible sound. As if someone might be there, examining the cup, or removing it.

Unmeasurable time hung in the cave. Its darkness swarmed with ghosts of sound, like the murmur in a man's ears of his own bloodstream. Like the unimaginable sounds inside an anthill whose inhabitants are seeking a way to climb out toward sentience. Growing louder now in the mind, a whispering that might have been blind cells; evolving, pre-conscious still, but desperate to grow, to find the long, hard way to Thought . . . .

This was becoming much worse than the dance.

Boris ached to leap up, to fight, to run away; but he made himself sit still. When the animal snuffling sounded again, it was almost a relief.

Now Boris could hear Red Circles coming to stick him again, behind the rocks to his left rear. It was a very faint sound of movement, but Boris heard it. How good it would be to turn around and smash the Sacred Rock into—

"Boris?" It was only the tiny ghost of a whisper, but he knew immediately that it came from Brenda. Great Gods of all the Themes! He wanted to whisper to her to get out of here, but his dry throat choked.

"Boris, it's Brenda. I can see, a little. Do you need water?"

"Yes," he got out, in a faint whisper. "But—"

She was moving away already, crawling in almost perfect silence, apparently going to get him a drink. She must be mad, completely mad. But what was he to do, call her back and start an argument?"

Then Jones's voice came again, from somewhere on Boris's right.

"Brazil, I did want to. I've thought it out, I've faced it."

"Jones? What's that?"

"I did want to give up everything. I sit here in the dark, and I can see into myself. I left Kitty, and I left my work, and everything else I had. I wanted to be a fanatic, to give up my whole life for something, and I did. For the Water."

"It—may work out." Boris could hardly understand what Jones was talking about. He was listening for Brenda, expecting every second to hear the sounds of her capture or murder. He wondered if any of the warriors who must be listening now could understand his talk with Jones. Quietly Boris stretched and flexed his legs, getting ready for the hopeless running fight that seemed inevitable now. At least such a distraction might give Brenda some chance to escape. But how had she got into the cave? and where was she?

"It'll work out, all right, Brazil. I'll tell you how it will. I gave up everything for the Water, and now it's given me up. I'm cured." Jones's voice was dead.

"What?"

"That last drink we had, starting this initiation business. It tasted the same, but it meant nothing to me—it had no effect. I'm dead, Brazil. My life has gone, for nothing."

Boris was listening and listening for Brenda, sifting every whisper of sound from the far reaches of the cave. He almost shouted for Jones to shut up. "Maybe so, Jones," he said.

"Maybe so? Maybe so? Listen, Brazil, they put a cup here, right in front of me. I wonder what's in it."

"They set a cup here too but I didn't taste it."

"No, you wouldn't. You're not the kind to give up your life for something. Nobody's ever understood me. Not my wife or anyone else. If I thought that this cup had the real Water in it, and that I might feel it again—"

"Can't you keep quiet?"

"Quiet? Quiet? Gods of Space, I'm dead, and you say keep quiet. All right, Brazil, I'm putting you back under orders, right now. Don't move unless I tell you, and don't lie to me."

Boris heard a faint sound behind me, and he knew somehow that it was Brenda coming back, bringing him water. He was afraid to try to move. His freedom had been only an illusion, and at a word from his master it had flickered away into nothing. Boris could do nothing for Brenda, or for himself, or for anyone else. Whatever happened was not going to be his fault, no, not this time.

Jones said, "Brazil, is your cup still there? Taste it and tell me what it is."

"I don't know if it's here."

"Boris." It was Brenda's whisper, from behind him. Boris realized suddenly that they must have given her the Water of Thought during the women's ceremony, and that it must have unbalanced her in some way. That was what brought her here now, trying in this mad fashion to help him.

Jones said: "Brazil, I order you."

"Boris." She whispered his name again, and this time one of the warriors heard her. Boris could vaguely see the man's upper body; he was passing nearby, turned at the sound of Brenda's voice. He stood for a moment without moving, probably incredulous, and then, soft-footed as a cat, came closer to investigate. In ghostly silence the warrior passed so near that Boris could see he carried a short spear, and was going to probe with the spear for Brenda.

Boris moved, without thinking of whether it might be possible — the terrible thing called freedom was his again.

He should have used the sacred rock, but for some reason he set it down before he rose up silently behind the warrior. Boris's left hand shoved low into the Kappan's back, ready to break his balance, and Boris's right arm whipped around in the silent-killing throat attack. Boris was stiff and weak; the man was not properly caught but retained balance enough to twist around and gasp in air, getting ready to yell. Boris drove knuckles into the man's throat, preventing any intelligible outcry, and then grappled for the spear.

A second later the silhouette of the warrior's head bent backward; hands had reached from behind him to claw at his face. Boris managed to wrench the spear away, spun it end for end, and drove it home. A dying weight sagged away, sliding quietly to the floor of the cave.

Then Brenda had Boris by the hand. She was kissing his hand and tugging on it at the same time, pulling him away. He let her lead him. The only hope now was to get out of the cave, and quickly, by whatever route she had used to sneak in. Other warriors must already be approaching to check out what had caused the scuffle.

Behind Boris, a far louder struggle exploded in the darkness. Jones's voice bellowed: "Brazil! There is no cure! Obey me! Fight for me!"

Lantern beams were springing alive, centered upon Jones. He had captured a spear, and was fighting like some mad Norseman. Another spear had already been thrust through his body. One warrior lay at his feet, while more of them closed in.

There was nothing to do but go with Brenda and get out of there. Boris followed her insistent tugging, away from the lights and the struggle, under an overhang of rock that forced them both down to hands and knees, on after that into still deeper darkness.

"Brazil, fight for me! I'll have the Water— before—"

Jones's voice died away, and the sounds of fighting with it. The faint reflected glow of the lanterns had now vanished entirely from Boris's vision. *Jones is cured*, he thought suddenly.

It was as dark as total blindness here. Brenda had released Boris's hand and crawled ahead of him. Now and then his hand, groping for the way, fell on her shoe or ankle. The way had now become a tight, low passage through which he was almost too big to scrape. He lost the rocks from his net-suit, and he lost a little more skin, but he got through, still gripping his captured spear. After perhaps thirty meters of this kind of crawling he could hear insects. A few meters more and the overhead suddenly receded. Raising his head he glimpsed a sliver of comparative brightness, like the night sky. And there, a star.

There was room now for him to move beside Brenda. "This way out is the women's secret," she whispered. "One of them showed it to me today. And I took some of their night-vision drug."

Now at last there was room for them to stand and walk; the secret passage emerged into the open air through an otherwise almost inaccessible hole in the rocky hillside. Only now did Boris fully understand, with dull surprise, that night had indeed fallen again; he had been all day inside the cave.

They were standing on a sort of rocky balcony, in

front of which a boulder made a crude, chest-high parapet. Anyone starting up the hillside from below would have a hard climb getting to them, and they were going to have a hard time getting down.

"We'll be safe here, for a while," Brenda whispered. "All alone." She put her arms around Boris and pulled his head down and kissed him fiercely. Then she let go of him abruptly. He could see in the starlight that her hands were busy with the front of her own coverall.

He was so stupid with thirst and fatigue and weary pain that for a moment he did not comprehend what she was doing. "What . . . ?"

"Boris, please. I can't help myself." She had started to take off her coverall; it was pulled down to her waist; and now Brenda threw an undergarment aside. "Here." She grabbed his hand and pulled it to her breasts.

"No," he croaked. Stupid as he was, he realized that it was the damned Thought-Water making her do this. She had been leaning toward loving him, and the Water had pushed her, as it had pushed them all. Anyway, the only animal urge he was able to feel at the moment was thirst. "Water," he croaked, looking downhill over the starlit forest.

"Boris! Boris?"

But he was already climbing over the irregular natural parapet. He scraped himself some more, but hardly felt the damage. Down under those trees somewhere was water, real water, cool and drinkable. He hadn't staggered far down the slope before Brenda was with him, her clothing more or less arranged again, holding his arm to keep him from falling on his face. "The river's this way," she said. Her voice sounded as if she might be weeping.

He was headed that way already; it was obvious
from the shape of the land where the Yunoee must
lie. He reeled toward it with only elementary
caution, and when he came to it at once threw
himself down on the bank. He thrust in his head, he
drank and wallowed. He emerged with a sharpened
awareness of all his pains and problems, but he felt
able again to think with something like clarity.

Brenda was lying beside him on the bank, waiting
for him. "Now, Boris. Please. Love me." Again the
coverall was open. Almost off, not quite. He understood with pity that she was trying to be as
provocative as possible.

"Brenda, not here, now now. I've got to run for
my life, they'll be out here after me any minute. It's
the drug making you do this now—"

She gave a little scream, pure suffering, as if he
had burned her with a hot iron. Her hand lashed out
to slap across his face. "You filth! I risked my life to
save you!"

"Brenda—" He hesitated. Was it worse to bring
her with him or to leave her here? Was her ankle
ready to stand a long flight? He didn't know how fast
he himself was going to be able to move, shoeless
and battered as he was. If she stayed here, and they
didn't know she had sneaked into the cave,
Magnuson might protect her; whereas if she fled
with Boris, and they were caught . . . but Morton
and Kaleta were here, too . . .

Brenda lay on her back. She spoke now in a sober
voice: "Boris, I tell you I've got to have you. I can't
help it. Otherwise I'll kill myself."

VII.

Boris scrambled to his feet and reached to pull Brenda up beside him. "Then come," he said, and kissed her quickly, once, and turned and trotted away, dodging among the trees as if flint points were already hurtling at his back — as well they might be, at any moment.

Brenda kept pace at his side. Her ankle must be healed, or very near it, or else she was ignoring pain — as he was. They ran in silence, saving breath. Once Brenda, with her augumented night vision, pulled at his arm to steer him clear of an almost invisible stump.

After a few minutes of this Boris halted, in a small clearing, breathing hard, long enough to get his bearings from the stars. Then they were off again. Boris had decided to set a course northward, at right angles to the easterly direction of the colony. Some of Red Circles' men were sure to be sent to the east, to get ahead of the fugitives and cut them off. Boris meant to go far enough to the north to get around them.

But the most immediately important thing to do was to put distance between themselves and the

JANET AULISIO © 1980

warriors' village. So far the grassy footing was fairly easy, and Boris meant to make the most of it. With daylight they would have to find a place to hide and rest; then he could think about improvising shoes as well as scrounging food.

Brenda, who had not spoken since he had pulled her up from the riverbank, still matched the speed of his long strides through the night. She at least had shoes on. But her ankle . . . so far she was giving no sign that it might be a difficulty.

More minutes had passed, and there was no sign of pursuit as yet. Now a small ridge of land cut across their way, and Boris, saving breath, indicated silently that they should climb it. Going up, he avoided any way that looked in the starlight like a path, for beside a trail on this rim would be an ideal spot for a sentry. Red Circles, he thought, you're going to have quite a chase before you catch us, giving us this much of a start. In fact you'll find to your surprise that you can't catch us at all—positive thinking is the thing.

At the top of the ridge they paused again for breath. Boris looked back along the way they had come, and reached to grip Brenda's hand tightly in his. Now there were torches visible among the trees; but the searchers' lights were scattered widely and uncertainly, and Boris and Brenda had several hundred meters on the nearest of them.

Her face was turned up to him in the starlight; an anxious, trusting face, very beautiful to him now. "Are you all right?" she whispered. "Can you go on?"

"I'm all right. Your ankle?"

"It doesn't hurt."

He was about to remind her that it was not too late for her to turn back and seek Magnuson's protection. But something in the way that Brenda was looking at him now reminded him of her pledge to kill herself if Boris abandoned her. "That's good," he said. "Come on."

He set a course along one side of the ridge, north into the hills. Brenda with night-seeing eyes chose the easiest path among trees and brush. Again they were silent as they traveled, and Boris used the time for thought.

As he read the situation, once the ordeal was over Magnuson would willingly join in the pursuit. When officially a member of the tribe he would be a great Kappan chief, and could have no tolerance for those who fled from baptism. That Morton and Kaleta, if they survived the test, would also join the chase was obvious.

His thinking seemed to be discovering nothing but new problems, not ways out of them. When the ridge they were following mingled with a jumble of other hills, Boris continued to direct their flight northward, angling a little to the east. Their pursuers seemed not to be prospering, for when he looked back from high spots he saw no more torches. But the real pursuit had not got started yet. The Kappans would probably wind up the initiation ceremony, and wait until dawn, before organizing an all-out search.

Now for a while north was downhill, and the going correspondingly faster. Presently they came to a stream. Boris was almost sure it was the Yunoee again, here upstream from the villages. Brenda

agreed with his judgment that there were probably
no more villages up this way; neither of them had
heard any mentioned. He drank deeply again, and
this time she drank at his side.

"We've got to keep going," he told her. "But first I
have to rest a minute." He sat down for a moment
on the grassy bank beside the star-reflecting
water . . .

A vivid flash of memory came, a picture of Jones,
fighting in the cave, his body transfixed by a spear.
Boris's head jerked up in alarm. He had dozed into
sleep, sitting slumped over on the bank of the murmuring stream; he woke now with his head pillowed
on Brenda's lap.

Gods of Space, he had more than dozed, the
eastern sky was gray! Boris jumped to his feet in a
near panic. He turned his head this way and that,
looking and listening, ignoring Brenda's soft protests
that she had been on guard all the time.

"You should have wakened me!"

"You looked so bad, so worn out. I was afraid
you'd collapse if you tried to go on without rest."

Muttering, he waded into the stream, and bent to
drink again.

The water here tasted faintly fishy. Well, what
was so strange about that? There were doubtless a
number of different things that could make a stream
taste fishy. Fish, for one.

"What is it, Boris?"

"I don't know. Nothing. Come on, we've got to
move. We'll travel in the water now."

Brenda followed him. The Yunoee flowed dark
and quiet around their knees, swallowing their trail

as they waded upstream. Boris stopped now and
then to bathe his stiffening little wounds. He washed
the dried Kappan blood from the spear that he still
carried.

Dawn was becoming a fact. Boris tasted the river
again. It wasn't just fishy; there was no use trying to
deny that here it savored faintly of the Water of
Thought. That was one taste that he was never
going to forget.

Tangled thickets nearby grew right down to the
water's edge. Boris probed his way with the spear
into the densest growth, where midnight gloom still
held. "There's a little space in here. We'd better rest
here through the day."

When with the second dawn the ordeal came to
an end, Magnuson with the other survivors returned
to a joyful welcome in the Warriors' Village. Their
wounds were treated, and the new members of the
tribe drank and ate and rested beside the old. The
festivities were marred and somewhat rushed by the
news of Brazil's so-far-successful flight. But before
allowing himself to think much about that problem,
to sleep, or even to relax, Magnuson had first to see
that the new man, the one-handed hominid, was
safely housed in the pen where he had been one of
six confined animals the day before yesterday.
Then, planning the new man's protection and edu-
cation, Magnuson fell asleep.

He was awakened by a not-too-gentle prodding.
Standing over him was a figure wearing a groundsuit. Startled, Magnuson jumped to his feet.

It was Morton's face inside the helmet.

"Magnuson, you're coming with me. They haven't caught Brazil yet, and we can't let him reach the colony, him, or Brenda either. I can run them down easy in this suit, if I can get on their trail. But I need some guides and trackers to do that, and I need you along to interpret. Also I want to keep you under my eye."

Magnuson thought about Brazil. It was too bad, but . . . "Yes, he must be caught. And I suppose the girl too."

"Damn right. I'm glad you see things straight for once."

Jane, excited, came running up to them. "I'll come with you, Don. I'll help."

"Woman on a war party? I don't think the spear-carriers would go for that."

"I suppose you're right." Jane was pale, breathing heavily. "But you'll catch them, won't you? Both of them, and bring them back?"

"You just a little jealous, Janey?" Morton grinned.

The young woman's face twisted into a mask of insane excitement; of hate, the like of which Magnuson had never seen on a rational human. Jane raised clawed fingers. "When I get my hands on her again . . . "

Magnuson, watching, felt a weary concern. He had too much to do, too many responsibilities. Jane and Brenda had both been given the Water of Thought for the first time, and he, under the press of other worries, had all but forgotten to consider the fact. Of course the Water was likely to have a drastic effect on their psyches. Not so great as if they were males, of course but . . . and Morton! Again

Magnuson was going to have to deal with a madman clothed in the power of a groundsuit.

Magnuson looked closely at Morton. "How do you feel?" he asked, carefully.

"Feel? I'll feel fine, as soon as I get Brazil in these." Morton raised the suit's armored hands, and smiled again. "You look a little surprised to see me dressed up, Doctor. Why, you told me the whole tribe would be my brothers now. Nobody stopped me putting it on."

"Will you two get going, then?" urged Jane, her fingers twisting nervously at her hair. "Catch them. Why should *she* ever have him?"

"She's right, Professor," said Morton. "Come on, let's get the show on the road."

"All right. All right, I'll come with you. Where's Kaleta? I'll have to leave some instructions with him."

"In there, still sleeping it off. Hurry up!"

Magnuson entered the indicated hut and shook the mayor awake. "Kaleta, can I trust you to do something important?"

"Uh. I can hardly move."

"You needn't move much. I've got to go off with Morton, for days perhaps. My hominid is in the pen, here in the village. I don't really expect any of the villagers to attack him now, but I want you to guard him, just in case. And give him food and water. It is supremely important that he survive. You must watch over him till I get back."

"Awright. When I wake up."

"You're awake now. You can move out there and sleep in front of the pen. No one will bother you."

From outside, Morton shouted: "Get the lead out, Magnuson! I'm taking a regular war party north! That's the way they went!"

But Magnuson persisted. Half-dragging, half-cajoling, he got Kaleta out of the hut and posted where he wanted him. Then there were a few other preparations to be made as rapidly as possible. Morton fumed, but had to concede grudgingly that the prospect of an extended march made them necessary.

Setting out at last with Morton and six warriors, Magnuson glanced back into the empty-looking village. Kaleta's plump form was stretched out in sleep beside the pen. Above him the one-handed hominid reached out through the palings, as if still asking some patient question.

Boris woke to find the sun near the zenith, one greenish glint of its surface coming through the close tangle of the thicket to strike him in the eyes. His head was on something yielding . . . not Brenda's thigh this time, but her folded coverall. The bare softness of her body lay curled and snuggled at his side. Last night . . . yes, last night.

The thicket was quiet. The river murmured just out of sight. Boris eased himself up to a sitting position, his cuts and bruises protesting fiercely. He was ravenously hungry, and reached out at once for a sample of the juicy stalk of a likely-looking plant. While awaiting his stomach's judgement on this morsel, and for Brenda to awake, he maneuvered himself into a crouching position under the close overhang of branches, and pulled off one of the small rocks still hanging to his net-garment. With this he set about quietly trying to detach the sleeves of Brenda's coverall, with a view to making himself some kind of footgear.

His moving around soon woke her, and she looked up at him unreadably. Even before she moved, she asked him: "Boris, do you love me?"

"Yes." He knew he was answering the Water. But what else could he have said?

Brenda sat up and looked at what he was doing. "Let me help you with that," she offered, having grasped at once what he was trying to do.

After a little discussion of the project he let her take over, and crawled about cautiously prospecting for more food. A few trees grew up through the thicket, and under the loose, shaggy bark on their trunks Boris discovered some grub-like things. These creatures were no doubt rich in protein and fat and the first one he sampled was quite palatable, at least to an experienced planeteer who thought about something else while swallowing. Brenda made a face at the idea of such fare, but then she wasn't really hungry yet. Boris wasn't either—that is, not approaching starvation—but he didn't need to let things go that far before he could suppress his civilized tastes. Today even raw and hairy food meant strength, and strength meant life.

Brenda did try some of the juicy plant, whose sampling had not as yet made Boris sick.

"I wish they hadn't made this damn thing so well," she muttered, working awkwardly with rock and spearpoint to separate the coverall's seams. Naked, crouching over her primitive job, she looked like a primitive herself. Not really, though.

"Hey."

She looked up, from under a tangle of soft brown hair.

"I do love you."

They ate a little more, and lay together once more and rested, and then worked again on the job of making footwear. At last Boris had, if not shoes, at least a pair of very tough socks bound onto his ankles with net-strings. The loss of the net garment didn't bother Boris much; it had provided neither modesty nor protection. Then they slept.

It was nearly dark again when they were wakened by men's voices, moving along the opposite bank of the stream, no more than ten meters away. It sounded like the villagers' language. The two in the thicket, he with spear in hand, she gripping a rock, waited silent and motionless until the sounds of speech had faded out into the distance.

"What do we do now?" Brenda whispered cooly then.

"Let's discuss."

It was nearly six days now, to the best of Boris's calculations, since Jones had pointed an energy rifle at him and compelled him to swallow the Water of Thought. It was a couple of days since the ordeal had started, and doubtless that had been over for some time. For nearly twenty standard hours Boris and Brenda had been free, a state of affairs that would not sit well with the Kappans, or with Magnuson, or with the smugglers either.

"The Kappans probably won't care a whole lot one way or the other about you," he whispered to

Brenda, watching her work her way as quietly as possible back into what was left of the coverall.

"I suppose; what's one female more or less? But Don Morton and our dear mayor will have other ideas." She reached for her shoes.

"But I think Magnuson is probably still in charge."

"Are you telling me I should give myself up?" Her fingers, ready to pull on a shoe, were still.

"No. Only that if worst ever comes to worst . . . your ankle's still swollen, isn't it? You're having trouble getting that shoe on."

"I can walk."

"We ought to be able to tie some kind of bandage on it."

They did. By that time it was quite dark, and Boris, spear in hand, led the way out of the thicket and into the river again. When he drank, he was again aware of the taste of the Water of Thought. It was faint but undeniable. This time he spoke of it to Brenda, and she agreed with him. Now was not the time to debate possible explanations. They moved on upstream.

Within a kilometer, as Boris had more or less expected, they ran into steep rapids. Here they had to climb from the stream; and when he stood on the high bank looking back he got a nasty shock. There were lanterns bobbing about near the thicket where they had spent the day. His plan had used up their strength and time, and had moved them a score of kilometers farther from the colony, but their pursuers were now as close on their trail as ever. Or at least some of them were. He had succeeded in

scattering and worrying his tribe of enemies somewhat, but that was about all.

There was a reasonable path here following the
course of the river, and he led Brenda upstream
along it. If they struck off through the bush now
they might slow themselves down critically and
would certainly leave a plainer trail. The sleeve-
socks were an enormous help; getting even this far
without them would probably have been impossible;
but Boris doubted whether they were going to be
enough. Tonight, he thought, my feet will give out
on rocks or plant-stubble somewhere. From then on
I crawl.

As before they spoke little on the trail, giving
them both plenty of time for private thoughts. Boris
looked up frequently at the stars. The cruiser had
been scheduled to arrive three days ago, and it
might very well be up there in orbit now. But then,
the difficulties of astrogation being what they were,
the ship might very well be three days more, or even
longer, in reaching the system. And when it did
arrive, and the people on board learned something
of the colonists' difficulties, they would hardly start
their search during the hours of darkness.

These were not very positive thoughts that Boris
was entertaining himself with, but they were the best
he could do at the moment.

It was a nightmare of a night. All through it, four
or five lanterns stayed on their trail in the dark, becoming visible whenever Boris and Brenda topped a
rise. At last the undergrowth beside the riverbank
trail thinned somewhat, and they could move away
from the river long enough to start a false trail or

two. These seemed temporarily effective; each took their pursuers a little time to figure out.

His feet. His weary muscles. He was debating with himself whether to try sending Brenda on ahead; and then he saw in the starlight how her mouth was set. Now when he looked at her movements closely he could see that she was trying to conceal a limp.

"Your ankle. I thought it was all right now."

"I must have given it another little twist back there. One of those underwater rocks. Boris, go on ahead. They won't hurt me if they catch me, you said so yourself. But they'll kill you."

He might have laughed, if his throat wasn't so sore. If several other things. "I'm moving at about top speed right now, girl. I was about to send you running on ahead."

After that there seemed no more to say.

At dawn there were no dense thickets to hide in readily available, and the last look at the lanterns had shown them so close behind that Boris dared not delay even a minute to look for a good hiding place. They were following the spine of a high, wooded ridge now, and they just kept moving along it. Boris considered going downhill into the ravine, hoping to find a wadable stretch of the Yunoee, or some other stream to drown their trail; but if he went foothill and then missed finding an escape, the hunters would be down on them like an avalanche. He didn't think that he could climb another hill.

Having just admitted that to himself, he saw a place just ahead where the ridge that they were following angled higher. A sketch of a path led upward, and in the soft dust were several sets of prints, from what certainly looked like bare prime-theme-human feet. He pointed a finger at them and croaked something.

"Boris, I can't make it." Brenda stumbled, tried to get up, then stayed down on her knees. "Go on. I'm going to try to hide."

If he tried to help her walk they were both going to fall down. "I shouldn't . . . " He wanted to say that he shouldn't have brought her, let her come along, however it had happened. Too late now. He bent over Brenda where she sat in the dust and they clasped their hands, all four of them, together.

He could do nothing for her unless he got away.

"They won't hurt me. Go on."

Actually he thought she was going to be better off being caught separately from him. He croaked some kind of a farewell and turned and tried the hill. Somewhat to his surprise he found that he could manage it, at least on this soft dusty trail. His feet had once been useful things, and he supposed they might someday be so again, but right now he would prefer not to know them. As for things like water and food and rest . . . rest . . .

He was getting lightheaded, and all he had to do now was faint and roll back downhill; that would fix everything nicely. Scion of the Martian Brazils, famous bon vivant and adventurer, adjudged not quite human by Red Circles, scion of the Kappan Circles . . .

Boris topped a small rise in the trail and stopped to breathe. Brenda had managed to get out of sight somewhere, he couldn't see her. He could see the warriors coming, though, only two hundred meters behind him now, and they undoubtedly saw him. There were ten of them, and one had something over his eyes as if to shield them from the light. So, one had taken the night-vision drug, that was how they had tracked the fugitives through the night with only torches and lanterns to light the trail. It seemed unfair.

Boris climbed on. He had to pause now at every second or third step to rest, and he looked back each time he paused. The warriors saw him, all right, for they pointed at him, and waved their weapons as if to urge one another on. But still they advanced only hesitantly, making no real speed. Could they possibly fear him? Did they think he had magic powers which had let him escape the ordeal?

Gritting his teeth and gripping his spear, Boris kept going. They weren't gong to take him prisoner, no, not again. His hunters continued to gain on him, but as it were reluctantly. Maybe from down there he looked like a man walking deliberately, contemptuous of his pursuers. Maybe if he turned around and walked toward them they would run.

He glanced back once more and nearly fell, for his hunters were indeed retreating, backing downhill with nocked arrows and leveled spears. Boris looked uphill, and saw the hominid troop coming down in a slow semi-circle, dozens of wild adults, armed with stones and crude clubs. He faced immediately toward the retreating hunters and hurled his spear after them, staggering with the effort. The spear fell ludicrously short, but the gesture just might suggest to the hominids that his heart was in the right place. About half of the hominid numbers charged downhill past Boris, howling at his erstwhile pursuers, who turned and fled. The other half surrounded him, yipping and jabbering about him, not knowing what to make of him. These were no dead-eyed quarry beasts. It seemed to Boris, groggy as he was, that these might very well be men. He made a planeteers' gesture designed for communicating with Apparent Primitives, and aroused some interest. The hominids formed a loose squatting circle around Boris, and took turns jabbering. They shooed insects, and panted and yawned, incidentally displaying their human teeth.

Boris's head was spinning, but he kept on making gestures, and tried a few words of this and that, being careful not to sound like a villager. His audience gaped unappreciatively. To blazes with them all, and also with the idea of preserving a show of something or other. If he was going to die here, it would not be while standing on these feet. He sat down in the dust, and by probing gingerly through the fabric of his improvised socks tried to decide how much was left of his soles.

From somewhere downhill came cries and shouts that sounded like a fight in progress. Most of the crowd lost interest in Boris and charged off in that direction. But half a dozen stayed behind, still watching him.

Should he try to tell them about Brenda?

First he was going to have to try to ask them for some water. Because the sun was so hot . . .

He was being carried, his head on a leathery shoulder, other arms and shoulders supporting his body. Hominid smell was thick about him. Over-

head, treetops flowed by at a fast walk. Boris's mouth was wet; it seemed that water had been poured on him, and he had a memory of recent choking and swallowing. It was dim here under the tall trees, though what little Boris could see of the sky was still bright with daylight. The trail he was on was narrow and twisting, overhung by many branches. His unspeaking bearers were carrying him into some secret fastness of the dim green forest.

VIII.

Capture, thought Brenda, had been something of an anticlimax.

The scowling warriors who had at last come upon her trying to hide in the woods had jabbered contemptuously. Obviously they were at first of two minds as to whether to take her into custody, or simply hurry on with the important part of the chase, ignoring the alien female with the flat forehead, close-set eyes, and what they must think of as disgustingly soft skin.

But in the end they had collected her, and one of the junior members of the party afte some protest had been delegated to lead her back toward the Warriors' Village. Once deprived of his part in the glorious chase, her disgruntled guard had seemed in no great hurry to get home, which was a relief. Brenda hobbled along in front of him as best she could, wishing that she had a crutch. And she thought about Boris as she went.

Looking back now, she was abruptly horrified at the memory of how she had acted on first getting him out of the cave, how close she had come to getting them both killed . . .

JANET AULISIO © 1980

But he knew what the Water of Thought could do; he would understand. After going through one day of it himself, Brenda wondered how Boris could possibly have retained his basic sanity through five.

Hobbling through the woods, almost back at the village now, she smiled, lightly and briefly, remembering that day in the thicket. There was something good to be said for madness. If you could only turn it on and off . . .

She had felt the madness and now she knew it for what it was. And she considered herself free of it now. And she would be ready this moment to rejoin Boris if by doing so she could be of any help.

He hadn't been caught. He hadn't been caught yet. There had been yelling on the trail ahead, immediately after they had separated, when Brenda had crawled off the trail and tried to hide. But those yells had not been cries of triumph, she was sure of that. And now, on her way back to the Warriors' Village as a prisoner again, another search party, outward bound, passed her and her escort. And the warriors in it were made angry by what her escort had to say to them. And, when no one could see her, Brenda smiled.

As with her capture, there was no particular excitement about her arrival, when she limped at last back into the village common, and was allowed to sit down there in the dust. The few children playing nearby took little notice. Nor did the women who were passing to and fro, stolidly engaged with their eternal chores. Brenda was one of the tribe now, and the women made friendly gestures to her across the barrier of language. They didn't mind that she had run away. Probably they had done that, or felt like doing it, themselves.

"Brenda!" It was Jane, her face showing relief, running toward her. "Brenda, honey. Oh, I'm so glad you're all right. You are, aren't you?"

"Basically. How about you? Where are the others?" Brenda let Jane help her to her feet, and lead her to a nearby log that served the village as a bench.

"Nothing's happened to me, honey. Except . . . Don went wild when Boris got away. Worse than any of the Kappans. He's out chasing Boris now, and Dr. Magnuson is too." Jane, her face troubled, sat down at Brenda's side. "Eddie was killed, in the ordeal."

"I know. I'm sorry."

"Yes. I don't think he'd have taken me offworld anyway. I think he had one of those permanent marriages." Jane pulled her arm from Brenda's touch. "Bren, I have to confess something. It must have been that drug that made me do it. When I heard that Boris had run away with you, I—I was hoping that they'd catch you. In fact I ran around here screaming, like some terrible . . . I wanted to see him *dead,* and you too, rather than see you with a good man I couldn't have." Jane began to cry. "I don't suppose you can understand. How could you?"

"Oh, Janey, it *was* that awful drug. I know. It—it made me do things too."

The two small town girls who had grown up together sat side by side, trying to comfort each other, both of them weeping.

"Where's Mayor Pete?" Brenda asked, finally, dabbing at her eyes and looking around the village.

"Lying around somewhere. He hasn't got over the initiation yet. I wish I'd never heard of him, or Don Morton either. I knew they were both rotten, and still I played along with them."

Pete Kaleta peered cautiously around the corner of the hominid's pen, looking across the village common at the two girls, who were now crying on each other's shoulders again. Probably they were set to talk and weep the rest of the day. They were not likely to interfere with anything he did.

The hominid inside the pen reached out through the palings to touch Kaleta's coverall; Kaleta brushed the single leathery hand away with distaste.

"So, you and I belong to the same club now," he said aloud, looking at the hominid. Both bore practically the same ritual wounds from the ordeal. "I hope you feel as lousy as I do."

The pale eyes looked back at Kaleta with what might be frustration, as if the creature wanted to talk to him, and almost but not quite knew how.

Kaleta turned away. Since the ordeal he had not been able to think for long of anything, not even his injuries, but one thing: what he had seen in the Temple Village, only a few kilometers away — a vat, filled with many liters of the Water of Thought.

The interstellar crime syndicate would pay a fortune, a vast fortune, for the contents of that vat. And now the warriors were gone from all the villages, Magnuson and Morton were gone too, Jones and Brazil were out of the way. There was no one, really, between Kaleta and all that wealth down in village.

And the copter was still parked in concealment down there near the Temple Village. Magnuson believed himself to have the only power key for that copter, but Magnuson was wrong, not as smart as he thought he was. Kaleta had hidden an extra power key inside the copter's cabin, and he had also concealed a weapon there.

It was not likely that Kaleta would ever get a better chance than this. He could walk downstream right now, go to the copter, and arm himself. Then he could raid the virtually undefended Temple, and fly away with buckets full of the Water of Thought. He would hide the stuff somewhere nearer the colony, and when the Space Force came he would put them on a false trail and try to keep them away from these villages. Of course there were great risks involved. But the possible reward was so great as to be worth any imaginable risk.

Kaleta saw himself safely away from Kappa and the wife who had gradually become no more than an irritation, amid the fleshpots of Earth or Planet Golden, maybe allowing a few of the more beautiful women there to help him spend some of his money.

He drew a deep breath, and found that his decision was already made. He would do it; he would gamble everything now. A helpful idea immediately suggested itself, and Kaleta smiled and opened the door of the hominid's pen. Let the creature wander away. Then Magnuson, returning here, might think Kaleta had gone chasing after the escaped hominid. Or, Magnuson might even blame the villagers for both disappearances. Either way there would be a diversion.

Without waiting to see whether the hominid took immediate advantage of the open door, Kaleta turned and walked calmly away himself, as if he was just going into the woods to relieve himself. No special preparations were necessary for his plan. The few Kappan women and children in sight ignored him; he didn't think Jane or Brenda were aware of him at all.

Once the trees were solidly around him, Kaleta quickened his pace. Going downhill, he hoped to be able to reach the Temple Village in two hours or less.

As he emerged from the woods onto the riverside path, he stumbled awkwardly, and cursed. He was still worn out, aching all over, from the ordeal. He had had only about six hours sleep before Magnuson awakened him, and very little since then. Plenty of reason to worry. His original plan with Morton now appeared hopeless. Morton in a groundsuit was another good reason for Kaleta to get out; he didn't trust Morton a bit. But overriding all details was the thought of that vat of the Water of Thought, and the price that the Outfit would pay for it.

He would get away with twenty or thirty liters if he got a drop; maybe he could get a lot more. He could force some of the Temple Villagers to help him carry pails. All Earth-descended men probably looked a lot alike to them, and he might easily manage to blame his actions on someone else. There were all kinds of possibilities as well as dangers in his plan; he would just have to work it out as he went along. But he could not turn down this chance of enormous wealth—because nothing else mattered, by comparison.

His legs were already weary, but still Kaleta walked quickly, sliding and scrambling down the steeper places in the path. As a member of the tribe, he expected no trouble from any Kappans he might meet. Even Magnuson halfway trusted him now, and that was the biggest joke yet. Magnuson was, must be, highly intelligent. And yet, blinded by his obsession with ordeals and weeding out the unfit, wanting to be God and decide who could live and who couldn't, creating men from baboons.

It was strange, thought Kaleta, how everyone among the Earth-descended except himself had been mentally twisted by their draughts of the Water of Thought. Jones, driven to give up everything else just to get another drink of it. Brazil curiously paralyzed in his will. Magnuson probably confirmed in his pseudo-religious fanaticism. Jane driven mad with envy of Brenda, and Brenda . . . Kaleta hadn't seen enough of her since the ordeal to know what the effect on her had been. And Morton . . . Kaleta hadn't seen much of Morton either, but enough to get the idea. He looked over his shoulder now and shivered slightly. Morton in his right mind was bad enough.

A collection of nuts, all of them. Psychos. It seemed that he, Pete Kaleta, was the only one who had not been unbalanced by drinking the Water of Thought. Probably that was because he was the only tough-minded realist among them to begin with.

Could he be that firmly certain of his own sanity? As he hurried downstream now he frowned, trying to step back mentally and view his present actions with complete fairness, objectivity. His basic goal, realistically enough, was wealth. Very well. Then it was perfectly logical for him to steal the most valuable property within reach (which happened to be the Water), hide it somewhere, and sell it later on. Of course, he repeated to himself, it was a dangerous plan, but you never gained anything important without taking risks.

After he had somehow weathered the inevitable Space Force investigation, the smart thing would be to smuggle the stolen Water offworld in small batches. That way the whole thing could never be lost at once. He had his contact with the Outfit. They would know ways. But he would have to be very careful that they didn't cheat him.

He would have to be careful in other ways, too. For example, about suddenly leaving Kappa to enjoy his new wealth. That would look very suspicious. If need be, he could forego the fleshpots and continue to put up with his wife's whining and nagging. Once wealth was his, nothing else would bother him greatly.

Maybe, with a little luck, Morton and Magnuson and Brazil would all eliminate one another. That would help a lot, if Kaleta didn't have to try to kill them himself, or cut them in. And the two young women would have to be put out of the way somehow; he had known them since they were just children, and it was sad, but there it was. They were all dangerous to Kaleta's wealth.

Anyway, back to the heart of the plan: when he had surmounted all such dangers in one way or another, he would smuggle his stolen Thought-Water off world in small batches. He would have his payment smuggled in, in installments, just as the Water went out. None of your electronic credits, not in this case. He wanted something more tangible. He would arrange to be paid in bills of high denomination, which would take up little space, and so could easily be hidden.

Puffing with effort, his feet hurting, Kaleta still smiled and maintained his rapid pace downhill. His vision of wealth, before vague and abstract, had now taken concrete form. He could almost see the money, the dozens of crisp bills coming into his hands. Possibly he'd get away with forty liters of the Water today, and possibly the Outfit would pay him five million for that much. Maybe just the first installment, for the first small batch smuggled off-world, would be half a million. He would bury it in the woods, probably, somewhere fairly near the colony. Interstellar currency was made to last, physically, and it would stay buried years and years without any special precautions and still be fresh and crackling whenever he went to dig it out and look at it and fondle it. Kaleta could almost see that first payment of half a million, maybe three-quarters of a million right now, he could see the numbers and the zeros on the bills—

A rock tripped him, and he sprawled painfully on the path, skinning the hands he used to break his fall, awaking pain in all his wounds from the ordeal. He cursed and scrambled to his feet and hurried on.

After he had stolen and sold this first barrel-full of the Water of Thought, collecting his first five or six million and putting it away, what was to prevent him from raiding these villages again and again,

getting away with more and more of the stuff?
Maybe the Space Force could be put off somehow.
Maybe he could bribe someone, even a Tribune.
Kaleta grimaced. He would try that only as a last
resort, for bribing anyone important would mean
giving up a substantial portion of his wealth. A
crooked Tribune would certainly be very greedy.
Kaleta groaned aloud, hurrying through the woods.
It seemed he was doomed to share his money, with
Morton or with someone else.

A sudden thought stopped Kaleta in the rocky
path, and made him face back upstream. The *real*
wealth, the source of the Water was somewhere back
up there. Immediately after the ordeal, he and the
other new members of the tribe had been told something of its secrets, Magnuson translating for the
others. Most of what had been revealed was magical
nonsense about this and that, but one real secret was
that the Water of Thought was obtained by raiding
the territory of the Forest People, north of the
villages. Kaleta had been too groggy then to think or
care about it, but now he saw how this offered unlimited possibilities for the future. When he had
weapons, and a copter, and time.

But the vat in the temple was a sure thing, and he
had better concentrate now on today's job. When he
had that vat emptied he could go on with further
plans. Kaleta faced downstream again, and hurried
on.

Now the Workers' Village was just ahead. A
branching trail joined in here, and along it a few
kilted Kappan men were approaching, dragging
with them a half-grown male hominid, gagged by a

stick tied into its mouth, its arms bound. The men
were laughing and pleased with themselves; evidently they had just caught a beast that would be
useful in the quarry. When they saw Kaleta they
stopped and stared at him, letting him pass the
intersection ahead of them.

He waved and smiled at the workers, as he would
have done on meeting Kappans near the colony. He
half-understood these villagers' speech, but now he
did not want to try to say anything. All he wanted
was to pass these men without alarming them.

He apparently succeeded in this, and in another
minute was entering the Workers' Village. The few
people he saw were, appropriately enough, at work,
and paid him little attention. Trying to look like a
man on a casual stroll, he stopped at the village well,
where the river water came up mudless after filter-
ing through twenty meters of sand. Taking his time,
Kaleta hauled up a bucket and then drank from a
gourd hung at the well. He smiled at some watching
children, and then walked on along the downstream
trail.

When he was a couple of hundred meters below
the Workers' Village, he looked about to make sure
that he was unobserved, then waded out into the
Yunoee. If he had all his directions straight, the
copter should be less than a kilometer from him
now. It was hidden at the edge of a landing clearing
in the woods on the other side of the river, just a
minute's walk from the Temple Village. Probably
there would be a Kappan guard or two watching the
copter, but Kaleta now had the wounds of the ordeal
to prove that he was one of them. The half-wit

fraternity, Brazil had said. Right now Brazil was probably wishing he had joined.

The river, nowhere more than a stone's throw wide, was not swift at this point. Kaleta did not even bother to remove his light boots, though he had to swim a few strokes near the center of the channel. Then he was wading again, reaching the opposite shore, and climbing out. The only people in sight were a few kilted laborers, and they were a long way off and paying him no attention. He walked away from the river, across a cultivated field, and then into woods again.

He located the copter's hiding place with little trouble. It was just a little natural clearing whose two or three obstructing trees had been hacked or burned away. The copter was just where Kaleta had last seen it—pulled a little way back out of the clearing, under high trees whose canopy of branches would make it virtually invisible from the air. There were two guards in sight—not fierce warriors, Kaleta saw thankfully, but a pair of robed priests who looked as if they did not know what to do with the clubs in their hands. Evidently Red Circles' men were all busy hunting Brazil.

Kaleta approached casually, and walked calmly out into the clearing. He smiled and waved to the priests when they saw him; though not very martial, they were muscular youngsters, and he was going to have to be careful.

"I must enter bird," he said—or tried to say—in their language, as he walked toward them. He pointed at the copter to show what he meant, and continued to smile.

The two regarded him with some dislike, he thought, but no real suspicion. They gave the impression of being uncertain about the duties of guards, and jabbered between themselves, saying something about the chiefs. Finally they made way for Kaleta to approach the copter.

Still smiling, he stepped past them. He opened the door to the cabin, and felt inside a small storage compartment under the front seat, letting out a breath of relief when his fingers located the machine pistol and the spare power key exactly where he had hidden them, taped to the top of the compartment out of the way of a casual inspection. There were also a couple of extra clips of ammunition for the pistol, which he pulled out and stowed in a pocket of his coverall.

Then he climbed up into the copter and looked over the controls. Everything appeared to be in order, ready to go. Now all he had to do was collect his cargo.

As he hopped down from the copter and approached the guards with the gun aimed, his hands were shaking. He had never killed anyone before, and he felt almost sick at what he was going to do now. But then he visualized the money again, and saw these two Kappans standing between himself and it. They would never stand by and let him load buckets of the Water of Thought and fly away with it.

The pistol made a low, ripping sound, like heavy cloth tearing. It was not very loud, but the two young Kappans were twitching on the ground, amid a great deal of blood. Kaleta saw that he had used up half a clip, and reloaded. Now his hands were steady. He dragged the riddled bodies into the bushes, out of sight, and kicked leaves over the blood.

So far, so good. Now, should he fly the copter into the village? Easier to get the Water aboard that way. But that would attract the attention of everyone in the area; and, Kaleta recalled, there were enough trees in the village to make it difficult at best to land. He wasn't all that great a pilot. He made sure there were no bloodstains on his hands or clothing, stuck the pistol inside his coverall, and started briskly along the path to the village. This was where Brazil in a suit had once confronted and disarmed him. Not this time, Brazil.

At one point along the path he had a good view of Great Lake, which was as calm as ever, rimmed by distant green hills under the greenish Kappan sky. Lake and hills and sky made a peaceful scene, and Kaleta stopped for a moment to look at it. He felt a twinge of yearning. Why did life have to be the grim and ugly thing it was? But there was no getting around it, the game of life had to be played by the rules of harsh reality.

He went on. A few seconds' walk took him past the spot where Brazil had jumped out in the ground-suit. Kaleta smiled.

His smile grew broader as he entered the Temple Village; it was, if anything, more nearly deserted than the other two settlements had been. Kaleta proceeded straight to the Temple and went in. He found no one in the first chamber. The door behind the stone altar led him into the room where the

Water of Thought was buried. An old priest and a young one were sitting on mats. They looked up as Kaleta came in, and were astonished when he went straight to the sunken vat and pulled aside its coverings. The priests both shouted angrily at him, and he drew the pistol, wondering if they even knew what it was.

The older man came forward, waving his arms and yelling. Kaleta shot him, knocking him back across the room. The young man just stood still, gaping, frozen with shock.

Against one wall was a neat stack of wooden buckets with fiber handles, clean and painted utensils. Possibly, thought Kaleta, they were the means by which the warriors who raided hominid territory brought back the Water of Thought. He grabbed up a pair of the buckets, one nested inside the other, with his left hand, and held them out. The young man remained frozen. Kaleta cursed him with no effect, and had to kick him a couple of times before he would start to move.

"Fill them! Like this!" Kaleta got himself a third pail, and dipped it into the opened vat. He would be able to carry only one himself; he had to keep the pistol ready.

At last the young man got the idea, and obeyed. Then Kaleta prodded him toward the exit. "Go on! No, stupid, take the pails with you! Carry them!"

A woman saw them come out of the Temple. She saw what they were carrying, and ran away screaming before Kaleta could decide whether or not to shoot at her. It was too bad, but he would probably have to do some more killing before he got away.

"Go—that way—go on!" Kaleta urged his coolie through the village. The Kappan moved ahead slowly, carrying his two buckets dripping with the Water of Thought, stopping every few feet to look back in unbelieving terror, as if he expected Kaleta to vanish at any moment. Kaleta snarled at him and jabbed him on with the pistol.

"Don't slop that stuff around, you—" But if he hit the man, more of the Water would certainly be spilled. They made slow progress, but fortunately the village remained empty, as if the only effect of the woman's screams had been to scare the remaining people away. It seemed to Kaleta that it took him an hour to urge his trembling, laden captive as far as the copter.

Luckily the young man had set down the buckets before he saw the four dead hands of the two guards that protruded from a thicket; at that sight, he went completely to pieces. Kaleta shoved him aside, and carefully hoisted his thirty or thirty-five liters of wealth into the rear of the copter, a pail at a time. He found a roll of sealing-plastic in the copter, and wrapped the pails to minimize any further spillage during flight. Everything was working out.

He hopped down from the copter, and was about to shoot the only potential witness who might be able to identify him, when there flashed before his mind's eye the picture of those other empty pails inside the Temple.

It was agonizing. There had been so much Thought-Water left in the vat. Should he attempt another trip? The delay meant risking what he had already gained.

Maybe he could make ten million today. Or even twelve. All for himself.

Instead of shooting the blubbering youth, Kaleta grabbed him by one arm and slung him staggering back toward the village.

"We go again. Hurry!" Kaleta made the youth run, and ran beside him. At the edge of the village Kaleta had to stop for a moment. He was still weak from the ordeal. If he fainted now—

But the vision of his wealth was plain before him, and he knew he would not faint.

"Come along, hurry!"

The village still looked empty of people; Kaleta gasped with relief. Only the old priest's dead body inhabited the Temple. Kaleta handed two more of the pails to his unwilling partner, and again took another for himself.

This time the Kappan youth knew what was wanted, and moved a trifle faster, filling the pails and starting off to the Temple again. He kept darting fearful glances at Kaleta's pistol, but he was starting to think again, and Kaleta watched him carefully.

Kaleta felt a rising certainty that he was going to be able to get away with it; he could almost feel and smell the money. From here on it was easy. Even if half a dozen warriors came at him now, he thought, he could fight them off with the pistol, and get away

They left the village and traveled the long-seeming path again, with its view of the calm lake. They were halfway across the landing clearing when Kaleta heard a boy's voice shouting. A half-grown

JANET AULISIO © 19

robed youth ran out of the forest near the copter,
Red Circles gasping four steps behind him. Kaleta's
porter set down his buckets and fell on his face. Red
Circles had a bow and arrow in his hands, small
things that it seemed a child might use for practice.
The angle was wrong for Kaleta; if he shot Red
Circles from here, some of the bullets might hit the
copter, and could drain priceless wealth from the
Water-laden buckets already stowed inside.

Kaleta sidestepped for a better angle. The bow
twanged, and the little arrow came so swiftly that it
was sprouted between Kaleta's ribs before he could
try to dodge.

He looked down at the arrow in surprise, found
that he could not breathe, and dropped his pistol.
He managed to set down his pail of the Water of
Thought without spilling any before he fell.

IX.

Don Morton dug in his metal-shod feet and with his servo-powered gauntlets took a good grip on the trunk of a sapling. He bent his legs, then straightened them, lifting, grunting a little at the tree's resistance. With a mighty ripping sound, roots snapping like shots, the sapling gave up its hold on the soil.

It was a satisfying feeling. Morton stood up straight, waving the tree in one hand almost as easily as a feathered wand. "There. I'm getting pretty good, huh?"

Magnuson was busy studying the rugged landscape through a pair of binoculars, and did not answer at once. He and Morton were alone, for the moment, atop a ridge somewhere near the hidden headwaters of the Yunoee, deep in hominid territory. The six warriors who had accompanied them here as trackers on the search for Brazil were out now hunting down an evening meal.

In Morton's view, Magnuson's behavior ever since the ordeal had been even more arrogant than usual, as if the professor deliberately wanted to anger everyone he dealt with, Morton in particular. Now,

JANET AULISIO © 1980

the scientist gave no evidence of having heard what Morton had just said to him. And Morton had spoken plainly.

"How about an answer, huh?"

At last Magnuson put down the binoculars. "If the other party's report is true," he said abstractedly, "the hominids could easily have killed him."

Talking about Brazil. Changing the subject without answering. Was this man trying to get himself killed?

"I SAID, I'M GETTING PRETTY GOOD WITH THE SUIT!" Morton roared, turning up his helmet's speakers to amplify his voice. "ANSWER ME! ANSWER!"

Magnuson heard him this time all right. He looked vaguely sick and uneasy. "I'm sorry," he said. "Very sorry. Yes, you are getting good with the suit. Better than Brazil was. When you find him, he won't talk to you the way he did last time."

"Damn right he won't." Morton took the tree in both gauntlets and cracked it over his armored knee, and threw the shattered wood away. "And I don't believe that the hominids got him, either. I'm gonna get him."

Brazil was the kind of guy who liked to get into one of these superman suits himself, and then push people around. Morton remembered Brazil disarming him, back in the Temple Village. And then Brazil had somehow escaped from the cave of the ordeal. Doubtless he had been laughing again as he sneaked out of that and ran away, while Morton had had to stay there, and suffer, and . . .

"I'LL KILL HIM!" Morton bellowed. Then he

remembered to turn the speakers in his helmet down again. "A rotten bastard like that. I'll break his arms and his legs, and then his neck, when I get these hands on him." Morton raised the steel fingers that trembled in sympathy with his rage; oh, this suit was a wonderful thing!

"Yes." Magnuson heaved a tired sigh, put his binoculars back into their case, and sat down on a log. "In another day or two we may find him."

"Any idiot knows that; we *may* find him." Morton mimicked Magnuson's voice; then he puffed out a sigh of his own, and let the subject drop. He wished he could reach a hand up inside his helmet and rub the back of his neck; he was getting a headache. He felt weary. There hadn't been much time to rest after the ordeal, and he had worked hard today, practicing with the suit, and climbing cliffs and trees to look for Brazil. And the world seemed to be against him, as it had always been.

Ever since the start of the ordeal, when he had tasted the Water of Thought, all the causes of just rage that Morton had been forced to endure in his lifetime had seemed to take on doubled force. The Water of Thought was good stuff after all, for a real man; it just made him see clearly the way things really were.

The Water had made Morton fully aware of all the injustices that had ever been heaped on him, culminating in the ordeal itself. And during the ordeal his rage had been so great and pure that for a while it had made him meek. Morton had endured the sufferings of the initiation with what amounted to calm patience, because that was the only way he

could survive to eventually enjoy revenge. When he
had finished Brazil and got back to the village,
Morton was going to look up the warrior who had
tormented him during the ordeal, and devise for
him some elaborate, slow, and particularly horrible
death. Morton wanted to spend a lot of time and
thought on that project, not to hurry it.

Thinking of his enemies, Morton, tired or not,
was unable to stand still a moment longer. He spun
around, pacing nervously this way and that, his
armored hands flexing.

"Oh, sit down," said Magnuson peevishly. "Better
save some of that energy."

That tore it. With the gorilla-strong arms of the
suit, Morton grabbed Magnuson and hauled him to
his feet. He aimed a backhanded slap at Magnuson's
face, but at the last instant pulled it, stopped it
almost completely. He was going to need Magnuson
yet for a while.

Magnuson fell back over the log. He lay there with
his mouth bloody, conscious but making no move to
get up.

"Why don't you stop making me mad?" Morton
demanded. "You just keep asking for trouble."

"I'll try to stop."

Magnuson's cold eyes were uncomfortable things
to face, and Morton turned away from him. "Where
are those goods?" he wondered aloud. "They're supposed to be hunters, and it takes 'em all day to catch
one animal. I'm gonna see what they're up to." He
trotted away down the hill, moving heavily.

When Morton was out of sight, and he was alone,
Magnuson struggled wearily back up to a sitting

position on the log. He spat out some blood, and tested his loosened teeth with tongue and fingers. It was a narrow, extremely dangerous path he had to walk with Morton, every moment, until the effect of the drug had worn off. And then? He could not shake the conviction that Morton would still be deadly dangerous in the suit. Magnuson would never be able to fully trust him.

And yet, Morton had come through the rite of passage, had proved himself a man.

Magnuson shook his head. Morton's case proved only that real men could do bad things—as the case of Brazil proved that apparently strong, complete men could have fatal, hidden flaws that showed up only under the X-ray probing of the ordeal.

Magnuson was certain that only by such ritual testing of all its men could galactic, or at least prime-theme human, civilization save itself from decadence. What ritual might be applicable or necessary to humanity in other themes—squid-like folk with tentacles were not the farthest removed from *homo sapiens*, and some forms were completely sexless—was an ultimately fascinating question, but far beyond the scope of his own life's work. He had dedicated, consecrated himself, to the cause of prime-theme Man, here and now, on Kappa. To help the cause, Magnuson had stolen and lied, and worked with the dope-smuggling scum of the very civilization he detested, making himself doubly a criminal in its eyes. He had interfered with fatal effect in Kappan affairs, and he would be prepared to commit worse crimes still—but if prime theme civilization survived in the galaxy, Magnuson felt

sure of being remembered as one of its saviors. And
again it struck him as ironic that two planeteers,
members of that civilization's elite Space Force, had
failed Man's test.

Magnuson remembered his first drink of the
Water of Thought, which he had taken about a year
ago. It had been part of his first initiation. Then, in
the peculiar Kappan way, he had become a shaman
without first becoming a member of a tribe. On that
day, immediately after he had taken the drug, while
the drums pounded and the chant soared, he had
seen with new and overpowering certainty how right
and necessary was the work he had already chosen to
do—to pull the Kappan hominids through the sieve
of testing, extracting from them the new branch of
humanity which some of them must be ready to
form. This mystical certainty had continued during
the four or five days it had taken Magnuson to arrange his own disappearance and flee to these
remote villages. Then, though he had never begun
to doubt his work, a certain transcendent quality in
his belief had faded. He understood now that the
drug had brought that quality about, and had given
him the courage that he might otherwise have
lacked, to act on his convictions.

But the truth of his convictions had in no way
depended on the drug. During his first weeks among
these villagers, he had taken a good deal of interest
in the Water of Thought. But he was more anthropologist than biologist or chemist, and in those early
days the Kappans had not trusted him with free
access to the Water-vat in the Temple. Soon his
work with the hominids from the quarry had

absorbed him, and he had thought less and less
about the Water. In fact he had never tasted it again
until just before the recent initiation, when all the
candidates drank. It had been a pleasant surprise to
find that his earlier draught had evidently given him
immunity; if that was the usual case with Earthmen,
the crime syndicate was due to suffer a disappoint-
ment, which made Magnuson feel somewhat better
about his indirect involvement with them.

Now, the Water of Thought interested him hardly
at all. On Kappa or on Earth, the key to Man's
future lay in his deliberate evolutionary selection of
himself, not in drugs.

He yearned intensely to get back to the Warriors'
Village, where the new man-hominid waited, newly
human intelligence in his eyes. Living proof, who
must convince the Space Force that Magnuson's way
was right! Oh, in the name of Man, if only Kaleta
was taking good care of the hominid!

Some distance below Magnuson, at the foot of the
ridge, the suited figure of Morton now reappeared.
The six warriors were with him, and one of them was
carrying game. There was water down there, a small
tributary of the Yunoee. It would make a good place
to camp for the night.

Morton looked up and waved imperiously for
Magnuson to come down. It might be fatal to irri-
tate Morton again. Magnuson stood up with a sigh,
and began to descend the hill.

The sun was warm above. It came and went on
Boris's eyelids as if perhaps moving leaf-shadows
intervened. Before he even opened his eyes, he tried

to remember where he was. He could tell that he was sitting on grassy earth, his back propped against a rough-barked tree. Oh yes, of course, the picnic. Brenda was so beautiful—

An unearthly voice jabbered nearby, and memory returned with a rush. Boris cracked his eyelids open cautiously. He beheld a daylight scene in the shady forest. Nearby and in the middle distance, a number of gray, two-legged forms moved about. None of them seemed to be paying him any particular atention at the moment.

Had they carried him here to be guest or dinner? He was still alive, which argued for the former. And they had given him water, which was also a most hopeful sign. Boris tried to think his situation over, before he moved so much as a finger, or even opened his eyes completely, while his accumulated physical discomforts were still soothed by inertia.

At least he had escaped the villagers, Magnuson, Morton and Kaleta. Of course Jones had died in the ordeal, and for all Boris knew the other Earth-descended men might have also. It would be ironic indeed if Magnuson were killed in the very ritual he loved so well and prescribed for all—but Boris couldn't really believe that he had been. Magnuson would survive if anyone did.

And Brenda—at the thought of her, Boris opened his eyes wide, and raised himself a little from his position against the tree. She was either crawling about lost in the woods or the Kappans had taken her. If Boris was going to have any hope of ever doing anything for her, he had to start from where he was, by first finding out just what these hominids intended to do with him.

A few of the gray figures noticed his movement, and heard the accompanying groan. They turned toward him with mild interest. There was nothing like a general alarm, no monkey-cry of alert. What jabbering took place was between individuals. Watching and listening, Boris got a strong impression that it was genuine though doubtless primitive speech.

This was a gathering-place, obviously, but he could not call it a camp. The hominids who had driven off the village warriors had been carrying rocks and dead branches as weapons, but here not an artifact was in sight. There was not a lean-to, a fire, a bed, a shred of clothing or an ornament. With only his sleeve-socks and the remains of his net-garment, Boris could feel overdressed among these leathery nudists.

On other planets he had seen primitive prime-theme people who lived almost this simply. Yet something was very different here. Something was wrong in this Eden, something missing. A small crowd had accumulated and was watching Boris with curiosity before he realized what the odd thing was. There were babes in female arms, and there were hominids who appeared to be not quite fully grown. But above the age of beginning toddlers, there were no pre-pubescent children anywhere in sight.

Maybe it was a school day.

Boris decided that if anything like a joke could still occur to him, he was probably not yet dead. That made it necessary to sooner or later try to get to his feet. Slow movement, with many grunts and pauses, interested his primitive audience but did not startle them. Not that he could have moved fast enough to startle anyone anyway. At last he reached something like his full height, and began a planeteer's routine of supposedly friendly gestures.

He towered, a bit unsteadily, over the crowd, whose taller heads reached just about up to his armpits. These creatures were of the same form as the quarry-beasts that Boris had seen — and yet they were completely different. Apart from any moral or intellectual problems posed, the others had struck Boris as repulsive. He would personally have preferred to be away from them, to look at something else. But seen like this, in their own world, the hominids did not strike him as ugly creatures. Somehow the thickness of their grayish, leathery skins appeared to be perceptible, and was not unattractive.

As he went slowly through the sign-language routines meant to demonstrate his admirable qualities of goodwill and fearlessness, Boris became especially aware of one individual in his audience — this was a male, taller than the average and probably a little older, if silver in hominid hair meant age.

The others seemed to make way for him, with slight and perhaps unconscious movements. Boris paused in his presentation and looked at this individual, who took the opportunity to toss something toward Boris. Boris found himself catching and holding the raw hind-quarter of a small warm-blooded creature.

The haunch did not smell especially appetizing, but at least it was fresh, and Boris's stomach rumbled approval. He made his best thank-you gesture, peeled away some fur, bit, chewed, and swallowed.

The food-giving one said something to Boris. Boris wished him good health in return. In his professional judgement, the odds that these were human beings had just risen enormously. Near-humans might use tools to fight and hunt; but when a dominant male went about handing out food instead of grabbing it, it seemed a good bet that the sometimes blurry-looking line at the border of humanity had been crossed.

But the prime-theme human slot on Kappa was firmly occupied by the villagers' species. That they were true prime theme was proven beyond doubt by their extremely close biochemical kinship with Earth-descended humans. On a planet as Earthlike as Kappa, theory predicted, demanded, evolution of life in the prime theme, with earthlike humanity at the top . . . but could evolution on Kappa have two heads?

Anyway, today's dinner was not where a planeteer was eaten, but where he ate. The raw meat tasted better than the grubs that Boris could remember devouring in a certain thicket—though not a whole lot better, actually. Boris stopped gesturing for the time being and attended to his food.

The food-giver, watching him, alternately smiled and frowned, as if he might be considering the obvious language problem. Or perhaps he was only stretching his face.

Before attempts at communication were resumed, a real monkey-troop alarm was called. The hominids all scrambled away in one direction, jumping and shrieking. The food-giver ran with the others, trying like any leader to get ahead of his followers as soon as he could be sure where they were headed.

The mass movement turned out to be not a flight or an attack, but a greeting. It seemed that a war party, or at least some all-male group, was returning to the gathering place. Boris could not recognize the individuals in it, but he thought it was probably the aggressive gang who had gone skirmishing after the village warriors. This was borne out by the fact that several of the arriving hominids were wounded, two of them badly enough to require their being carried by others. One of the two had a disabled leg, and clung to a stretcher improvised from a springy branch. The other one looked dead.

There was a great deal of jabbering on all sides, and Boris was almost forgotten in the excitement. He noticed that the dead hominid was receiving more attention than the wounded ones. This struck Boris as odd, and he moved to a position where he could watch what was going on around the corpse. He could pick out no chief mourner, but it seemed to be an indignation meeting.

People as primitive as these were probably basically quite non-aggressive. Still it made Boris uneasy to be the lone outsider around when they were angry about something. It was a time to be unobtrusive, though not too timid; and that was a balance hard to strike, for a man who stood two heads taller than the crowd and came from a different planet.

But Boris, to his relief, found himself almost ignored for the moment. Here came a man with an edged stone in his hand, and Food-Giver beside him, making their way through the small crowd around the corpse. They both squatted down by the head of the body, and the man with the rough hand-ax went to work on the neck.

This was intriguing. Boris watched closely, with a hardened planeteer's interest. He thought he could guess what was coming next, for he remembered the hacked-open hominid skull that he had seen in Magnuson's laboratory near the quarry.

By now there were nearly a hundred hominids gathered around the dead man, watching. But Boris's height still let him see. The head came free, and was more or less peeled. Then the man with the hand-axe turned the skull upside down and attacked the base, enlarging the *foramen magnum* to get at the brain.

Boris was expecting an immediate ritual cannibalism of the brain. But to his surprise nothing of the kind was performed now. He missed some details of what was being done, but what he did see astonished him. Perhaps half a cup of clear liquid, only faintly tinted with blood, was drained from the skull into a gourd held ready by Food-Giver.

And that appeared to be that, for the present. The crowd gradually began to disperse. Boris saw that some of them were weeping, but this did not surprise him as it almost certainly would have a few days earlier. Here, after observing the hominids in their natural state for only minutes, he had seen and heard enough to convince himself of their human status.

The question was, what had been drained into that gourd, and what was going to be done with it now? The clearness of the fluid suggested lymph; Boris wasn't at all sure of the details of hominid physiology, except that it must be somewhat different from his own, and even from the Kappan villagers'. Boris had a wild and horrible suspicion about that clear liquid.

Some of the females were now gathering closely about the dismembered corpse. Boris did not wait to see what they were going to do with it. Wincing along on painful feet, he followed Food-Giver and a couple of others who were walking away with the gourd.

They took it without ceremony a couple of hundred meters into the woods, to a small clearing centered by a smoldering pile of logs. The grass near the logs had long since been burned away. A faint, worn path surrounding the blackened area showed that there was more or less regular foot traffic here. Possibly lightning had once fired a dead tree, and the embers had been fed and maintained for some unguessable time since then.

At one side of the blackened area stood a crude, kneehigh cairn of rocks, and a couple of hominids were already pushing a portion of the smoldering fire in that direction, scooping with sticks and leading the fire to the base of the cairn with a lure of fresh, dry wood. Others in the group had gathered large, thick leaves, which were now wrapped around the gourd. Then the gourd was settled on the cairn. Its exact positioning took some time. Boris thought it was left too far from the fire to cook, but where it would be heated. One man squatted down nearby, concentrating carefully on the fire's progress; the other hominids drifted away.

Boris found himself ignored for the time being. He was thirsty, and limped downhill, following the lay of the land toward the probably location of a watercourse. Though he had no plans for immediate flight, it was reassuring that no one hindered his movement. Before he started once more for the colony he meant to eat, and rest, and do something about improvising shoes, if not pants—the sleeve-socks had probably saved his life, but they were not what you could call adequate footgear for hiking.

At the foot of the slope, only a few score meters down, he came upon the small stream that he had expected to find; he wondered if it was the upper Yunoee. Boris lay down at the edge of it and drank, and felt a chill as if he had seen a great snake about to strike at him from the water. This stream was, though much diluted, undoubtedly the Water of Thought.

The stuff could hardly run in every river on the planet, or it would have been found long ago by Space Force people or colonists. So this must be the Yunoee, or a key tributary. The farther upstream, evidently, the stronger the taste. Down at the villages, it was indistinguishable from ordinary river water. What would be found at the source?

Boris took off his sleeve-socks and sat for a few minutes, cooling his sore feet in the stream, and telling himself that mere survival in his situation presented enough problems without trying to do exploration and research as well. But he could not shake the idea that here, especially, knowledge and survival were connected. At last curiosity won out, and he tied his footwear on again and began to hobble upstream along the bank. After a couple of bends in the watercourse he could see a waterfall not far ahead, a high slender curtain of crashing spray.

Studying the bank on behalf of his sore feet, Boris's eyes spotted an arrowhead; then another, a few steps farther on, half buried in dried mud. It was more than likely that Red Circles' men had once been here.

Now, looking for more clues, he could see in a nearby bush a broken pail, with a rotted handle of twisted fiber. Where had Boris seen the like before?

In the temple of the lower village, he remembered. Pails like this one had been stacked in the room where the vat of the Water of Thought was buried.

He stepped into the river, and bent and tasted it again. The unforgettable flavor was there; now it seemed to be growing stronger with every few meters he advanced, to the very foot of the waterfall. But still it was a flavoring only, not the strong Water itself.

Climbing the rocks beside the fall was a tricky job, but Boris was determined. He took his time about it, and at last gained the highest rock and sat on it, getting his breath, nursing his feet, looking ahead on a level at a green meadow of Eden. Above the narrow fall, rocks held the river back into a long,

sinuous spring-fed pool, enclosed on three sides by a
park of stately trees. When he had rested briefly,
Boris stood up and walked through the lush, well-
watered grass that rimmed the pool. All was so
peaceful that he thought of serpents.

It was no serpent's head that rose from the grass at
the very edge of the water. The head was that of a
half-grown hominid, who had evidently thrown
himself down to drink.

Boris made a peace gesture. The boy stared back
at him for long seconds, then rolled over toward the
water and drank again, as if still deeply thirsty.
Boris wondered if he might be sick. He was the
youngest-looking hominid, except for infants and
beginning toddlers, that Boris had yet seen in the
forest.

The youth took his time about drinking. At last,
with a sigh and a gurgling belch, he rolled back to
look once more at Boris. Something in the book
brought back the snaky chill Boris had felt on discovering what the stream just below the waterfall
contained.

Now Boris stepped carefully toward the upper
pool meaning to taste it. But for all his caution, the
young hominid was alarmed. The hominid was a
gaping boy no longer, but a startled ape, leaping up
heavy with drink, grabbing a fallen branch as
weapon, hooting and snarling wordless threats.
Boris stood still.

In response to the noise, another hominid torso
rose from the tall grass on the other side of the pool,
this one showing the budding breasts of a young
female. She hooted a questioning response to the

JANET AULISIO © 1980

male. She too had obviously been drinking, for silvery drops fell from her chin.

Boris stood quietly waiting. He was not physically afraid of the two small ones, but he wanted no misunderstanding with the tribe. Soon, the head of the girl on the other side of the pool bent down again to drink. But the young male on the near side was not so easily placated; he still crouched, baring his teeth and growling at Boris, a dog, an ape, an animal.

Then a thing happened that was perhaps one of the ordinary miracles of the universe; but Boris was to remember it with perfect clarity for the rest of his life. A critical synapse closed, perhaps, somewhere in the hominid brain; or some other threshold was reached, some other trigger clicked. The hominid body stood a little straighter, and a human being looked out of the hominid eyes. The boy distinctly spoke some words, which sounded to Boris like a slowed-down version of the adult hominids' jabber.

An answer came, from not far behind Boris. He whirled; Food-Giver stood there, a club held with apparent absent-mindedness in one hand. Food-Giver was a head shorter than Boris, but his limbs were heavily muscled; Boris had a rough moment or two before he could be sure that Food-Giver was not annoyed with him.

The young hominid dropped his own branch, and sighed. He gave the impression of having understood Food-Giver's words, and being reassured by them. Then he sprawled prone again at the edge of the pool to drink.

Food-Giver stood quietly watching Boris. Cautiously Boris stepped to the edge of the pool, bent, and put out a hand toward the calm surface. It seemed that he was committing no offense. He cupped up a few drops in his hand, and tasted; it was the Water of Thought, nearly as strong as what he had been forced to drink from Jones's stone bottle, and again before the ordeal.

Boris sighed, and started away from the pool, heading slowly downhill out of Eden. If he was allowed to, he meant to do nothing but rest and think and eat and drink for a day and a night. He was very weary and there was much to think about.

Food-Giver tossed aside his club and walked beside him.

X.

Getting food, as long as he was willing to accept what the hominids thought of as food, posed no particular problem. The moment Boris showed interest in anything that an adult hominid had and considered eatable, some of it was sure to be handed him. It was not, he observed, that he was being regarded with any special favor; the hominids did the same thing constantly among themselves. It was not surprising in such an extremely primitive culture. Food-Giver had probably achieved what dominance he had simply by being a better provider than anyone else around. The other side of the coin was probably that there were drawbacks to accepting too much charity, and Boris made sure to dig up some food for himself, lest he lose all status before his career in society could get off the ground. He even managed to give away a couple of juicy roots, and a few fat grubs that he felt no reluctance to part with.

At night the tribe bedded down under the trees, mostly paired male and female. Boris found himself a comfortable spot near the edge of the fire-clear-ıg, and when he woke during the night made

himself useful and kept warm by adding a log or two
from a pile that other people had brought in. The
leaf-wrapped gourd still waited on its cairn, and he
was careful not to disturb it.

It was morning, and Food-Giver was prodding
Boris awake. Grunting and stiff, Boris arose from his
grassy nest, and saw at once that something
important must be going on. Four or five of the
graying elders of the tribe were inspecting the
gourd.

Evidently they decided that whatever purpose had
made them put it by the fire was now accomplished.
It was handed to Food-Giver; and he, surrounded by
the irregular honor guard of the others, took it off
through the forest. Boris's feet were feeling a little
better this morning, and he kept up with them.
They looked at him curiously, and talked about
him, but made no objection. Actually he thought
that Food-Giver at least was pleased.

By a roundabout way that avoided any steep rock-
climbing they reached the pool of the Water of
Thought, above the waterfall. Food-Giver waded
out a couple of steps and poured into the pool, carefully but without any ceremony, half the contents of
the gourd. Then, using as dipper another gourd that
was handed to him, he added Water from the pool
to the original vessel until it was once more full.

Now the path to the fire-clearing was retraced; a
gathering of the younger adult males awaited the
elders and Boris there, and things were solemn.
Attention was centered on the gourd in Food-Giver's
hands. Boris, noting some serious looks directed at

himself, was willing to fade into the background, until even sharper looks and some jabber made it obvious that he was expected to stay.

There were no drums or chants here. Still, what followed now was certainly ritual, the first that Boris had observed among the hominids. The young men sat down in a circle facing the leaders; Food-Giver motioned Boris to take the place at the end of the young men's line. Food-Giver then solemnly handed the gourd to the man at the other end, who took a sip and passed it down. Each man sipped in turn, and the gourd moved down the line from hand to hand.

Well, it hadn't killed Boris before he knew what it was; and there was no way to avoid it now. When the gourd reached him, Boris was ready. He touched his lips to the stuff inside.

It was the Water of Thought, and, as far as he could tell, nothing but. Far stronger than he had ever tasted it before. What was the connection between the clear Yunoee and the lymph inside hominid craniums? Almost absently, Boris handed the gourd to Food-Giver, who had walked over to stand directly in front of Boris with what might be termed an expectant expression.

Food-Giver gently pushed the cup back, then raised his own empty hands in a pantomime of a man draining a drink to the last drop.

Well, Boris's second deep draught, just before the ordeal, hadn't seemed to affect him at all. What with his drinking from the tainted river, he might be building up an immunity. There was a good cupful left in the gourd, and like a good diplomat Boris drank it all.

The taste was not bad, really, but it was very strong.

With that, the meeting was abruptly over. The members of the council with one accord returned to their individual problems of digging roots and scratching parasites. Boris, finding that his hosts had begun to share with him other things than food and drink, made his way again to the river below the falls with an idea of drowning some of these gifts or persuading them to leave.

After some moderate success with that job, he hunted up a good flint point among the wasted arrowheads along the bank, and started to get some tough green bark from a tree. He had rather enjoyed planeteers' survival school; he thought now he might try his hand at making himself some moccasins.

Before he even got as far as peeling the bark for them, he knew he had a fever which was rapidly getting worse. He tried to keep working for a time, but then gave up and threw himself down in the shade; he was not only burning up, but getting light-headed. Damn the Water of Thought, you thought you had it beaten, and then . . . Jones, too, had been feverish from drinking a lot of it. What now, plenty of bed rest?

He tossed restlessly on the grass, wondering if he ought to go back to the river and try to cool himself. What a mad shivering chill that would produce. Someone came to sit beside him, and he looked up to see Food-Giver.

"I hope you can talk soon, Swimmer-With-Berries," Food-Giver said.

"Soon, but I feel sick," answered Boris, abstractedly, speaking the hominid language. The jabber felt strange on his tongue, and yet not strange. Then Boris sat up straight, gazing in awe at Food-Giver, who looked back in mild alarm.

"Great Gods of the Galaxy," said Boris softly, in Space Force-Colonial. There were no hominid words for that.

Fortunately the fever leveled off before he became delirious, though all he was able to do for it was lie in the shade and hope. Food-Giver and a revolving delegation of other adults stood or squatted around him, now and then questioning him softly and mournfully—or rather, questioning Swimmer-With-Berries, who had died yesterday from a villager's spear thrust. Boris of course was still Yellow Monster, his original self, but as the newest male around he had been chosen to bear the reincarnation of Swimmer too.

Boris fairly well understood all these things without asking about them, for he found himself now possessed of a profusion of hominid memories in addition to his new knowledge of the language. And yet, fever and all, he knew himself still as Boris Brazil; there was for him no real confusion of identity, no sense of any alien personality crowding him inside his skull.

Food-Giver (which was a correct title) and the others asked polite questions of Swimmer-With-Berries. Was he comfortable now? Had it been painful, they asked, to die?

No, it hadn't been, Boris remembered. Not very.

He could plainly recall looking down at his own gray
leathery chest, watching his own spilling blood,
glimpsing near his feet, where his failing hands had
dropped them, the rocks he had carried into the
fight. Vaguely he remembered seeing the
grotesquely tall, pale-yellowish monster who had
thrown a spear at the villagers following him.

Much farther back, he remembered himself at
other sessions like this one, asking the traditional
mourners' questions of the newly dead, who through
the Water of Thought were merged again with the
living.

But it was Boris who remembered all these things.
Squatting around him now were not old friends
talking with Swimmer-With-Berries, though they
thought of themselves that way. They were in fact
still Kappan hominids talking to a Mars-born,
Earthdescended planeteer. As Boris saw it,
Swimmer was dead and gone, but now parts of his
memory had been implanted like segments of
recording tape in Boris's brain.

Like cronies at a wake, Food-Giver and the others
chatted of old times, growing more cheerful as the
conversation moved along. Boris could not recall
many of the events they spoke of, and this did not
surprise them. That was the way the Water worked;
some parts of the life of the departed one were
always lost to death.

But Boris now had Swimmer's memories of many
everyday routine things, of eating and mating and —
on comparatively rare occasions — fighting. And
Boris now searched those memories for information.

There was a scene in which the dead body of a

young female was being ritually buried. Rows of hominid faces looked at Swimmer as his hands scooped earth into the grave where food and flowers had been placed already. There had been tears on Swimmer's face, but there was no emotional content now for Boris, in this or any of the other memories.

The earliest of Swimmer's memories that Boris could find was one in which he lay beside the Sacred Pool, drinking and drinking. His belly was already bloated with the Water of Thought, but it was still pleasant, even necessary, to drink more.

Of course. Young hominids after being weaned ran free in the forest, on the fringes of the tribal territory, surviving there as best they might. No adult tried to teach them anything, for they were not yet real Thinking People. They were Dark People still, like other animals. And sometimes the hated villagers trapped the young ones, and took them away to a terrible place where they were tortured, and made to spend their lives in moving stones. There they remained Dark People as long as they lived, because they were kept from the Sacred Pool.

At about the same time that a free young wild one grew into the power of sex, the taste of the Sacred Pool, which had been repugnant, suddenly became irresistably attractive. For long days the young ones spent most of their time lying by the banks of the pool, drinking until their bellies bloated, hardly leaving the place even to seek food. Then there came a time when the taste of the Water no longer pleased them greatly. Then they came and joined the tribe, bringing with them the powers of speech and thought, and the tribal memories.

The tribal memories?

Why, of course.

Now that he thought about it, Boris could easily remember himself in a female hominid body, gathering sweet roots along the base of a great ice wall that blocked the upper end of a valley . . .

As a planeteer, Boris could recognize the great ice wall as a glacier. But his Kappan memory brought back the looming size of it, and made him feel again its cold breath on his leathery skin, as if he had passed it yesterday.

Might that memory be ten thousand years old? Boris knew that at least that much time had passed since glaciers last scoured these subtropical valleys.

Restless with his persisting fever, and with the awe of what was happening to him, Boris got up and walked unsteadily away from the mourners. He made his way own to the Yunoee again, and splashed its fresh water on his fevered face. The Yunoee was cool, but Boris could find no memory of its ever being frozen, not even when the glaciers were near. All adult hominids knew that its Sacred Pool had to be defended. It was the Water of Thought, a River of Thought that flowed in the brains of men, generation after generation.

After drinking of the Thought-tainted water — there was nothing else available to drink — Boris scooped up a shaky palmful and held it close to his eyes. It looked perfectly clear.

Hypothesis. A microscopic organism of some kind — call it the X-bug — lives and thrives and reproduces in the Sacred Pool, and perhaps nowhere else. Some X-bugs are naturally carried out over the

waterfall, but for some reason they die or lose their
potency as they drift downstream; after a few
kilometers, only the fading taste of them is left.

A hominid drinks from the pool. Suppose that the
X-bugs resist digestion and are taken live into the
drinker's bloodstream. Suppose that they have an
affinity for the brain, and suppose further, if it is not
too feverish a thought, that they become a loosely
integrated but necessary part of the hominid brain,
serving some critical synaptic function and also
bringing information that is henceforth available to
the hominid as memory. And also, while in the
brain, they record at least some part of what the
hominid experiences.

Boris discarded his handful of water and started
groggily back uphill. He rather liked his theory.
There were the planarian worms of Earth, one of
which could acquire part of the simple learning of
another by eating the educated one's minced body.
There were analogs among lower forms in the other
common themes of known Galactic life.

How did the X-bugs manage to keep storing up
new data, century after century, and still retain at
least something of the very old information from ten
thousand years ago? Perhaps the X-bug
reproductive process started out each new individual
with half its data-capacity blank.

Boris was not a biologist, only a feverish and
beaten-up jack of all trades; but he thought that his
theory could not be too far from the truth.

The doctor, back at the colony, had said that
Earth-descended humans and the Kappan villagers
were remarkably alike, biologically. But after all,

Earthfolk were not meant to imbibe their memories and the neural connections of their speech centers. So when an Earth-descended person drank the Water of Thought, the X-bugs rushing to the brain found no ready welcome; they just raised frustrated hell there until eventually the body's defense systems did them in. A Kappan of the villagers' species who drank the Water probably experienced much the same thing in milder form — they spoke of going into trance under the Water's influence, and tapping racial memories. But it was small wonder that the Water of Thought should cause mental imbalance in the Earth-descended.

The mental effect of Boris's first drink had been so overwhelming that he had noticed no particular physical effects. But Jones had been feverish. Come to think of it, Jones had said things suggesting that he had picked up at least a few hominid memories with his draughts of Water. Then, after four or five days, both of them had recovered. Boris had regained his freedom, and Jones had discovered that the object of his fanatic passion no longer satisfied.

Perhaps their first drinks had given them a certain immunity, for their second drinks, at the beginning of the ordeal, had seemed to have little or no effect. Kaleta and Morton on the other hand had taken their first drinks only when the ordeal started, and therefore were probably still crazed in one way or another.

And Brenda — Gods, he had to get out of here and help her, or at least find out what was happening. But at the moment Boris was very glad just to be able to reach his shaded nest again, and sink down weakly into the grass.

"I am sick," he told Food-Giver, who was still waiting nearby. Food-Giver grunted sympathetically, and offered him half a mouse. Boris waved the gift away and closed his eyes.

Why should the third drink have sickened him, if he had been immune to the second? Well, for one thing, the third drink had tasted much stronger than the other two, and for another, he had been forced to swallow more of it. If his theory was correct, that third drink had brought X-bugs to his brain in such concentration that the data they carried somehow became available to him. Such close biochemical coordination was not unheard of between two races or species of the same theme from different worlds. Skin grafts could be made to take from Kappan to Earthman, Doc back at the colony had said . . .

But this time, though the drink had been stronger, Boris had not been mentally unbalanced by it. Maybe his psyche had actually been strengthened by that first bout of temporary madness—another intriguing theory. The Water of Thought was going to keep a lot of research people busy for a long time.

Magnuson was, or had been, a scientist of reputable standing. But he had swallowed the Water, and then apparently had never tried to work on it, to solve its puzzles.

Wearily puzzling about Magnuson, Boris fell into a fevered sleep. The mass animal-screeching of animal children awakened him. Swimmer's memory knew that particular sound, though faint with distance, to be an important warning, and it brought Boris jumping up from sleep. His first clear impression was that he felt much better. His fever had broken, and he was in a cold sweat.

Boris ran with other members of the tribe toward the distant sounds of alarm, picking up a club as he went. A couple of adult scouts who had gone out to investigate an earlier outcry were already hurrying back with their report to where the tribe was assembling.

"There are six villagers coming this way," one reported.

"And another monster, like this one," said the second scout, pointing to Boris. "And yet another monster, who is even stranger. It has no face or hair, but shines all over like the sun on water. They are all coming this way in a group, along the river, four or five shouts from here."

Food-Giver turned slowly to Boris, silently asking for expert advice on the subject of monsters.

Boris's fever was gone. If his theory was correct, the last living cells of Swimmer-With-Berries had been repelled from Boris's Earth-descended brain, and were food for phagocytes in his alien circulatory system.

But Boris found that he still understood the hominid language. With a moment's thought he could still recall the image of the glacier, though perhaps some of the detail had been lost. Evidently his own brain had somehow re-recorded much of what Swimmer's cells had tried to bring to it.

"I know this monster-who-shines," said Boris. "I think he and the other monster have come to find

me and kill me."

"If they come with the villagers, they must be our enemies, too," said someone. There was general agreement.

Boris was thinking that whoever was in the groundsuit could hardly be a real expert in its use. And would doubtless be demented in some way by the Water of Thought. Mentally tilted in some aggressive way, probably, since he came hunting.

Boris asked the scouts: "Did one of these monsters have shaggy hair on his face and head?"

"Yes, the one who did not shine had much hair, darker than yours."

Magnuson. Which meant that either Morton or Kaleta must be in the suit; and Morton was the tough-posing one. If it was true, as it seemed to be, that the Water of Thought pushed an Earth-descended man toward his weakness, Morton might well be afflicted with blind rages. This suggested a plan; it was rather a scary plan, and Boris looked for another one. Unfortunately without success.

He interrupted a strategy conference to say: "This shining monster is a very great fighter. Clubs and little stones will not hurt him."

There was an awed murmur at this; all eyes were turned on Boris.

Swimmer's segmented memories were unclear about something, and Boris asked for information. "Food-Giver, have The People ever attacked the villages?"

Food-Giver was perhaps astonished at having to explain any historical matter to Swimmer. But he was tolerant of monsters, and finally answered:

"Yes. The last time was six father's-times ago."

"If we go to fight in the villages, the villagers will kill us," observed another large man standing nearby. There were grunts of agreement. The Sacred Pool meant humanity to future generations of The People, so it would always be defended to the death. But what good reason was there for going to fight in an enemy village?

"I think that today all their warriors are busy in other places," said Boris. "And if we go to the villages we will frighten their whole tribe very much, so tomorrow their warriors may stay home instead of coming here. But first there is the shining monster to think about, who may kill all of us if we let him."

Again there was murmuring; but Swimmer's word seemed to be trusted.

"I wanted two of you young men, the most agile, to come with me," Boris said. "We will fight the monster among the high rocks, two shouts below the Sacred Pool." It was a bend of the Yunoee that Boris's eyes had never seen, but he could remember how it looked. "Then the rest of The People can easily drive off the six warriors and the other monster."

The Home Guard was much astonished; they were not at all used to such strong suggestions. For fanatically poor discipline, this army would have made Old American backwoodsmen look like Prussian regulars. Still, this proliferation of monsters was an unheard-of situation, and Boris's try for leadership was therefore at least tolerable to The People.

"We know six villagers are coming this way," said

Food-Giver, sticking conservatively to facts. "Maybe there are more. I'm getting ready to fight." He made no appeal for others to join him, had no comment on the plans of yellow monsters. He might have argued jealously against such plans if his culture had been slightly less primitive, but leaders in the simplest human societies everywhere rarely argued. Everyone did much as they pleased, anyway.

Boris called firmly for two volunteers. "You," he said. "And you. Will you come with me? And will you do as I say? We will have a hard fight, and a strange fight, against the Shining Monster. We will save many of The People from being killed."

The two young males he had chosen had youth in their eyes, as well as in their supple bodies. They came with him. They knew no more of groundsuits than of quadratic equations, and quite likely he was going to get them mangled; but he told himself it was for Brenda. And for The People, too.

XI.

"Now something's gone wrong with the damned suit," growled Don Morton, standing knee-deep in the swift rapids of the upper Yunoee. The suit's left arm had developed some kind of a hitch in movement; he couldn't control it precisely any more.

Magnuson, breathing heavily with his effort to keep up with Morton, was ascending the steep riverside path. The six village warriors were all out somewhere ahead, scouting. Or more probably loafing, Morton thought.

"I said, there's something gone wrong with this!" Morton waved the defective arm.

"Yes." Magnuson nodded agreement. It was easy to tell what he was thinking, though.

Morton demanded: "I suppose you think I shouldn't have broken all those rocks back there. Well, they kept slipping under my feet. Why shouldn't I hit 'em?"

"You know more about the suit than I do," said Magnuson.

"Damn right I do."

Morton climbed a little higher, enjoying the way the water roared at him, and couldn't push him

back, as long as he had solid footing. He paused, scanning the hillsides around him. Here, the hills were very steep, the bones of rock thrusting up through the soil, into occasional crags and pinnacles. Brazil could be hiding out right here, somewhere, thinking himself safe. Oh, to catch one glimpse of Brazil, who was the cause of all this effort and trouble! When he got a grip on Brazil he was going to tear him into handfuls. Slowly.

Magnuson had stopped to drink from the river. When he arose from the bank, he had a funny expression on his face; he smacked his lips, and looked thoughtfully upstream.

"Well, you got any more bright ideas?" Morton demanded.

"At the moment, no," said Magnuson, at once giving Morton his full, polite attention. Magnuson wasn't really such a bad guy; ever since Morton had slapped him he had been polite and respectful. It just showed that people needed a bit of rough treatment every now and then; it was good for them.

Morton got a drink, too, turning his head inside the helmet and sucking insipid water from the suit's small tank. Blah. Maybe he should chance taking off his helmet, so he could get a real drink too.

"Look! There!" Magnuson was crouched, his arm pointing, body tensed.

Morton whirled, sending up a spray of water. A few hundred meters distant, a figure moved along a steep hillside. An Earthman, tall and blond and nearly naked.

Morton hesitated momentarily.

"Go after him!" urged Magnuson. He straight-

ened, groping for his binoculars. "There's something burning between those little hills near there—
see all the smoke?"

"So what?" Morton took some slow steps in the
direction of the distant figure. "I'm gonna get him!"
Rage came to a focus. Running, the suit's legs
ripped sheets of water from the river. Morton
sprinted up the steep bank, smashing aside brush
and saplings, his eyes fixed on his enemy who was at
last in sight. The figure of Brazil soon vanished
behind some rocks, as if he had seen Morton
coming. Morton exulted. Go on, run, try to get
away! This time, I've got the suit!

Running in the groundsuit was an athlete's dream
come true, a joy that Morton experienced more
keenly with every trial. Almost effortlessly he now
made the first rough hillside flow down past him.
Rocks spurned by his heels flew back like missiles.

He pounded along the top of a rocky ridge for
fifty meters or so, heading toward the broken hills
and pinnacles among which Brazil had vanished.
Something was indeed burning there, something
sizable to judge by the size of the smoke-pall that
hung between the rocky hills.

Was Brazil trying to send up a signal? Morton
stopped momentarily, anxiously scanning the sky.
There were no copters in sight, no Space Force
shuttle craft.

Was the smoke, then, part of some kind of trick?
But he was invulnerable! Morton laughed aloud,
and flew on. At the end of the ridge, he recklessly
broadjumped a ravine; misjudging his landing on
the other side, he fell, sprawling and sliding halfway

down the next slope, among rocks. He was unhurt, but even a second's delay was maddening. Cursing and scrambling, he got himself reoriented and rushed on.

Here, he was sure, was the very spot where he had last seen Brazil. And now—there he was! The tall, unmistakable figure was hurrying away along a dangerous rocky slope, toward the heaviest smoke. Morton could see now that the dark gray clouds were rising from a row of fires, banked with smoldering greenery, arranged along the foot of the hill. Did Brazil really hope to confuse him with smoke? Morton laughed again at the futility of such a plan, and launched himself after his enemy.

Something struck with a sharp clang against his helmet. On the precipitous slope above Morton, a hominid snarled and jabbered, hurling down fist-sized rocks at him.

Morton growled in rage and charged the hillside. Sand and loose gravel flew out from under his metal feet; he fell, then slid down into the greasy-looking smoke.

The air inside his helmet stayed fresh—as fresh as it ever got—but now it was difficult to see. Again, a thrown rock clanged from his suit. He saw no one, but he could hear the chittering of his enemies plainly. As if they were laughing at him.

Were a whole group of hominids helping Brazil? That was fine with Morton. It would simply mean more targets for his revenge. He stood up, trying to see through the smoke, smiling coldly. Let them laugh all they wanted, let them think they might make fun of him and then escape. He could afford to let them laugh a minute longer.

Rocks pelted around him, here and there into the burning brush. As long as he stayed down here he could see almost nothing.

He climbed, carefully. But when he emerged from the smoke he found that he had got turned around somehow, and was on a different slope from the one he had slid down. Over there was the hominid, still in sight — but over here was another one, atop another peak. Morton tried to make up his mind which one to go after first, while more rocks clattered insultingly around him. As soon as he started after the nearest hominid, he heard a shout behind him. Brazil was there, up on another pinnacle, hurling rocks like an ape himself. So! Hominids forgotten, Morton reversed himself again. The shortest way to Brazil lay straight through the fires. But when he had kicked his way through the smoldering piles of brush, he found that the suit's faceplate was fogged over with greasy soot and adhering dust. Looking out through it, Morton could hardly have distinguished a crouching man from a boulder. He stopped, fumbling around inside the suit. There should be a washing system for the faceplate.

A hominid raced by, running like a mountain goat not ten meters away, and with a shriek hurled some kind of filthy muck at Morton. It spattered all over him, and part of it hit his faceplate, obscuring his vision even more. Morton roared, and gave chase. But where had the ape gone? He couldn't take his helmet off to clean it, they were pitching those stones much too accurately. But he had to stop for a moment and get his faceplate cleaned. Forgetfully, he brought his left arm up in a wiping motion, to try to scrape off some of the mess. The erratic arm smashed against the faceplate glass and the helmet just above it. That did it. In a frenzy, Morton pounded his own helmet again and again, with raging fists. The suit-builders had turned out junk, useless junk!

But the helmet and faceplate withstood the beating; and when Morton's fury had abated enough for him to finally locate the interior control for the washer, even it still partially worked, cleaning half of his faceplate.

He looked up, and was just in time to see Brazil, rolling a boulder down at him. With a yell, Morton charged. He meant to catch the rock and hurl it back, flattening his enemy like an insect on a wall.

The rock hit him before he realized that it was too big to catch, on this loose footing anyway. The boulder bore him downhill, and he screamed in terror as it bounded with him, spinning and rolling him helplessly among other rocks, shooting him finally against immobile masses of stone, with a clanging like the end of the world.

In an awkward position, almost standing on his head, Morton lay gasping for long seconds, before he could feel sure that he was not killed or maimed. In fact, he gradually realized, he had hardly been hurt at all. Just bruises here and there, and the wind knocked out of him.

"I'm gonna break your arms and legs, Brazil, and then your neck!" he called aloud, when he had got back on his feet at last. The threat sounded weak

and somehow inadequate to his own ears; but he was
almost incoherent. He knew his enemies were right
up on one of these hilltops. They would be laughing
at him, as they got ready to roll down more rocks.

Both sides could play that game! With a sudden
inspiration, Morton picked up some small rocks,
and looked around him for a target. Now where was
Brazil? It was almost impossible to see anything
clearly through this smeared and damaged
faceplate. Morton would like to get his hands on the
madman, the degenerate, who built this suit, and —

There was a hominid, looking down at him,
gesturing what must be insults. Morton threw an
egg-sized stone. It seemed to go like a bullet, but it
missed the target, whizzing off harmlessly into
space.

He could swear he heard them laughing. They
would be getting more boulders ready to roll down
on him. He started climbing; he had to come to
grips with them. He picked up half a dozen throwing
pebbles, but then his maniacal left arm dropped
and scattered them, halfway up the slope. Another
rock hit his helmet. Smoke drifted around him.

Morton was beyond rage. He made a crooning
sound, like a lover singing. When he saw Brazil, he
charged at full speed paying no heed to anything
else. A wide chasm was almost under his feet before
he saw it. Morton leaped desperately, and the edge
of the far side struck him in the chest. He clung
there with his arms, emptiness under his feet, and
the suit's left arm failed him again just as Brazil hit
him with another big rock. Then Morton was end-
lessly falling, bouncing and falling again, with the

world of rocks and sky spinning around him and suddenly going dark.

"Is the shining monster dead?" one of the young men with Boris asked him.

Boris had sat down shakily, collapsed would be more like it, on a ledge. His hands were bleeding from the edges of that last rock, and his chest was heaving. It had been a very near thing.

"I doubt it," he answered, when he could afford the breath for speech. "But I hope he will be hurt at least. Enough to make him stop fighting us."

"It will take—" The hominid held up a hand against the course of the sun. "This long, for us to climb down there and see whether or not the monster is dead. If the river does not carry him away. I think he finished falling in the river."

"You are a good fighter, Yellow Monster," said the other hominid, climbing up to join them.

"Thank you. Both of you are good fighters also. Let's just leave the Shining One where he is. I want to lead some of The People downstream now against the villages."

An hour had passed since Morton had gone charging away after Brazil. Magnuson was crouching behind a log, still within earshot of the murmuring Yunoee. The six village warriors were scattered around near him, also in concealed positions. Shortly after Morton had left, another band of hominids had appeared, and launched a stone-throwing attack, but the villagers' arrows had driven them off.

Some yelling had come from the rocks into which Morton had charged, but now all was quiet. Could Morton be still venting some fiendish vengeance upon his enemy? Or had Brazil out-thought him and escaped, or even found a way to defeat him?

Magnuson rather suspected the latter. It was hard for Magnuson not to admire a man of Brazil's capabilities. Maybe Brazil hadn't simply broken and fled from the ordeal. Perhaps there could be some deeper reason.

Magnuson, when Morton was dashing off an hour ago, had been on the verge of calling some final warning after him, a caution to be careful. But Magnuson hadn't called. It probably would have been a waste of breath anyway, at best. But also he must have been hoping that Morton, the proven man, would somehow be eliminated.

"Magnuson, someone comes."

The whispered warning roused him from deep and troubled thought. Around him the warriors were stirring cautiously, turning their attention downstream, to the south. Were the hominids trying to encircle and trap them? But Magnuson felt sure that such tactics would be beyond them, in the wild state.

And it was Red Circles who came into view on the riverside path. He was leading a comparatively strong war party, twelve or fifteen men, and as they came into sight Magnuson saw that all were carrying the painted buckets from the Temple. This, then, was meant to be a raid after the Water of Thought.

Red Circles came forward, walking tall, a bow and arrow in his hands, his eyes scouting the woods and cliffs. He stopped, and Magnuson stood up to greet him.

Reserved triumph, and perhaps amusement, were in Red Circles' eyes. "Magnuson, the Earthman Ka-le-ta is dead."

"What? How?"

Red Circles put a hand to his belt and pulled out a machine pistol, holding it awkwardly by the barrel. "Ka-le-ta violated the Temple, and he killed three men with this. So I killed him."

"What of the hominid-man?" Magnuson asked. "Be careful with that weapon; it is dangerous." He couldn't see if the safety was on. Kaleta must have had the pistol hidden somewhere; and he had still been dragged by the Water —

Red Circles curled at his lip at the mention of danger; but he held the pistol out to Magnuson. "Maybe you can kill some of the Forest People with this, Magnuson, though you have no skill with the bow. Maybe you will kill your hominid-man, for he has run away." Now the triumph in Red Circles' eyes was plainer.

"Run away?" Magnuson took a step forward, almost grabbing at Red Circles. "Where? How do you know?"

"The pen stands open."

Red Circles would not lie, but his tone was insolent. Magnuson accepted the pistol put the safety on, and stuck it in his belt. Then he drew himself up.

"Red Circles, you will speak to me with respect. The Spirit of Man speaks to this world through me, and that is a greater thing than you can

understand." Magnuson understood that there was
no Spirit, no God, and there would be none until
Man had evolved himself upward to infinite power.
But Magnuson's work brought that moment closer,
so he was not lying to Red Circles. Red Circles had
perhaps some dim appreciation of all these things,
but he could not know them as a civilized man knew
them, so their weight was all with Magnuson.

The war chief scowled, but he was still unable to
look Magnuson in the eye for very long.

"We must find the man-hominid," Magnuson
said firmly. "He is one of our tribe now. Have you
any idea where he is?"

Red Circles gave the Kappan equivalent of a
shrug. "Who can say where one of the Forest People
might hide?"

"We must search for him."

Red Circles shifted his feet uneasily, but his voice
was stubborn. "I and these men are busy, and the
men who were with you here are now going to have
to come with me as well. We are going to get more
Thought-Water. Kaleta defiled the vat, and the
chief priest tells me it must be restocked at once. So
we are going all the way upstream, to the Sacred
Pool. Once you asked many questions about the
Water of Thought, Magnuson. Now you are one of
us, and you can learn all about it."

This time it appeared that Red Circles was not
going to knuckle under. Still it was plain that he
wanted no quarrel, that he was trying to persuade
Magnuson. Once Magnuson would have needed no
persuading; he would have made a great effort to
discover the source of the Water of Thought. Even

now, the idea was tempting. This would be his last chance for any such discovery, for tomorrow or the next day the Space Force would be here, and he expected to be under arrest.

But there was no time to spare for any purpose but the most important one.

"We go downstream," said Magnuson, putting his full authority into his voice. "We must track down the man-hominid, and keep him with us. He is alone and confused, and I can understand why he runs away. But he is the proof of a very great magic, much more important even than the Water of Thought; he is a man made from an animal!"

All Magnuson's authority availed him nothing. "You go downstream, if you want," Red Circles said. "But *I* am chief of all these warriors." He turned, and shouted commandingly to his men: "We go up!"

Boris was beginning to suspect that he just might, after all, be the dynamic-leader type. He had now persuaded about twenty-five of the younger hominid men to follow him downriver against the villages. The two who had fought the Shining Monster with him had come back to the tribal gathering-place unscathed, and had been a great help in recruiting, with their tale of an easy dance through combat following Yellow Monster's instructions. It was against all the Space Force rules, of course, to exacerbate local warfare, but Boris could see no other way to go that offered so good a chance of getting his pursuers off his neck and perhaps even of rescuing Brenda. He was gambling that only a few villagers would be at home, that those who were

there would flee, and that casualties on both sides
would be at a minimum. He would gamble more
than that to help Brenda.

"Run forward and make much noise when we
come to the first village," Boris told his company as
they were setting out. "And remember to look for a
female monster; she is my friend."

His boys grunted cheerful assent; following a
determined leader was still a new and exciting game
to them.

When they got to the Warriors' Village they
charged whooping downhill, with Boris in the van,
and took the place by surprise. As Boris had hoped,
there was not a warrior home. The women and
children all evacuated the huts with miraculous
speed, and went screaming panic and murder down
the path toward the Workers' Village.

Thankfully there was no real murder, or even
injury; the hominids were not culturally advanced
enough to enjoy pillage and rapine. They shrieked
good-naturedly to urge the fleeing enemy on, and
waved good-by with clubs.

"Remember, look for female monsters!" Boris led
a hut-to-hut search, aided by those of his irregulars
who chose to help. It did not take long to make sure
that Brenda and Jane were elsewhere. Nor was there
any sign of Kaleta.

All this was fun! The hominids were ready to
follow Boris downhill again.

"We will frighten another village!" he shouted en-
couragingly, waving them on. He had a hard time
keeping up with them now, though he had stopped
to borrow a pair of some warrior's new moccasins,

which were an excellent fit, or at least felt like it after the sleeve-socks, which Boris now joyfully discarded. Shoes were a higher invention than the wheel, and he meant to insist on the point at the next scholarly meeting he attended.

Boris and his small, leathery army swept into the Workers' Village to find that panic had preceded them, and the huts and workshops were already empty of people. From the direction of the quarry there came a querulous hominid yipping; not words, but the frightened monkey-call of the young, though here in deeper, adult voices.

"It is the Dark People," said the hominid standing nearest Boris. In the next instant he ran toward the quarry, yipping a response. The others all cascaded after him.

"Wait! Not yet!" Boris had not foreseen this. "We'll get them out of there, but not yet!"

He might as well have shouted to recall the wind. His army was gone. But he could not blame them.

Seemingly alone in a deserted village, he ran from hut to hut.

"Brenda? Jane!"

No one. No answer.

In one hut he noticed a quivering mass of bedding, but pulling it aside uncovered only an ancient and terrified villager.

Boris took the downstream path again, this time alone. For the thousandth time he scanned the empty greenish sky for any sign of rescuing or searching copters. Nothing. There was no use expecting any help beyond what he could give himself.

As he neared the Temple Village he studied the

banks of the stream closely, and its shape. He was
looking for the pool where Magnuson had ordered
him to throw in the second groundsuit, and the
energy rifles. The suit might well be full of mud by
now, but Magnuson had not realized that an energy
rifle would not be fouled by submersion.

He recognized the pool at once when he came to
it, and waded out into the dark water, searching the
muddy bottom with arms and legs. The current was
not particularly strong here, and what he was looking for could not be far away. Unless someone had
beaten him to it.

Boris went under water to examine the deepest
part of the bottom. When he came up for a breath,
Morton was standing on the bank twenty meters
away, still wearing the battered suit, Number One.
He was watching Boris.

"The river's not going to hide you," the suit's
speaker said.

"Are you still drugged, Morton?" Boris asked.
And just then one of his groping feet found the
second groundsuit on the bottom of the river. Neck-
deep in water, he stepped back, moving his feet this
way and that, searching further.

"Oh no," said Morton calmly. "It's worn off. I
won't knock myself out anymore. But you know too
much about our little business now, I can't let you
stay alive. You and the others can be blamed on the
Kappans."

"Where's Brenda?" Boris asked, as his foot con-
tacted one of the energy rifles. His actions concealed
by the muddy water, he scooped up the rifle with his
foot, into his hands. But Morton was still too far

away.

Morton smiled. In a clear pleasant voice he announced, in obscene fantasy, just how he had disposed of Brenda. In the next instant Morton rushed Boris, charging with resistless speed into the water. He came on so quickly that Boris fired without raising the rifle above the surface.

A needle-jet of steam leapt up, at a sharp angle to the surface, and the groundsuit sounded, loudly, like a struck gong. Morton fell forward in a great splash as Boris dove out of the way. The suited figure floated, face down, hissing, and Boris could feel a wave of warmed water pass with it. On the back of the cuirass, where the power lamp rode, a blackened place the size of a saucer now showed; the suit's radio would be useless now, even if a way could be found to get at it.

Holding the rifle, Boris climbed again from the river to the path, and put on again the moccasins he had left on the bank. For a little while, before the suit started to sink and wedged in shallows, he and Morton kept pace toward the Temple Village and the vast, quiet expanse of Great Lake that lay beyond.

When he reached the third village, he found that the wave of panic sweeping before the supposed hominid onslaught had emptied it just like the others. Again Boris walked among deserted dwellings, shouting uselessly for Brenda and Jane.

Pete Kaleta's head greeted him from atop a crude wooden pole newly fixed in the ground just in front of the Temple. With shaky relief Boris made sure that there was only one such pole. Brenda and Jane

JANET AULISIO © 1980

and Magnuson still remained unaccounted for.

Boris entered the Temple, and poked his head and his rifle into the inner room. Four trembling priests stood there before the Water-vat, clumsily holding spears more or less leveled.

Boris had as yet been able to absorb next to nothing of the villagers' language, but he tried.

"Woman!" he said, or meant to say. "Woman. Me. Mine." He swept an arm around in a great gesture, asking where.

At last one of the priests appeared to get the idea, and raised a pointing arm.

JANET AULISIO © 1980

XII.

Red Circles and his augmented raiding party were out of Magnuson's sight now, on their way upstream. Magnuson, alone, was walking in the opposite direction, going downhill, back toward the familiar territory around the villages.

He had now been living and working in and around those villages for approximately a year. As he walked, he could see this rainy season's first towering thunderheads in the eastern sky, and he recalled that last year's rainy season had just been starting when he staged his disappearance.

There were times when he wished he might have devoted his life to some science as impersonal and plain as meteorology. But the Spirit of Man had called him, and he had been given no real choice. He had been forced to spend much of his life out of touch with the busy worlds of galactic civilization, to bury himself at last in these remote hills on this backwater planet. He had dedicated himself to his work, committed crimes in its name, was now hunting for a man to kill him to fulfill the demands of the ordeal. It would seem to most people a strange way to serve the cause of Life. But it was not really

237

JANETAULISIO© 1980

strange when you saw it clearly. Death was a necessary part of life. Failure had to die in order that
success might live.

Prime-theme galactic civilization had much to
learn, or re-learn, about the need for a continuous
weeding-out of its members. In his heart Magnuson
welcomed his approaching arrest and trial.
Whatever the exact charges might be, he meant to
make his defense an indictment and a lesson for
civilization.

His defense was going to be basically an
explanation of his successful work. He had raised an
ape-like, gibbering thing to the rank of Man, and in
the end the courts would not be able to deny the
living evidence of that one hominid; sooner or later,
the work of refining and perfecting humanity would
proceed, on every prime-theme planet, and that was
all that ultimately mattered.

Sooner or later; ultimately; but his own successful
defense was going to depend on his one living man-
hominid, and he had no guarantee that that one
creature was still alive.

As soon as he came in sight of the Warriors'
Village, Magnuson paused, sensing something
wrong ahead. The village was too quiet, it looked
too empty. There was no smoke of any kind.

There was a crackling in a nearby bush.
Magnuson turned alertly; it was only a couple of old
village women who had seen and recognized him,
and were now emerging from hiding. In excited
voices, sounding almost gleeful, they began a
jumbled tale of great massacre and destruction by a
thousand raging, wild hominids. The raiding horde

had been led, they swore, by the very same yellow-haired, Earth-descended man who had so magically escaped from the ordeal.

Magnuson soothed the women as best he could, and tried to find out some hard facts. That proved to be impossible, or nearly so. Then, despite their dire warnings and refusals to go with him, he hurried into the depopulated village. No corpses and no damage were visible; but hominid droppings were visible in several places, testifying to a core of truth in the women's wild story. Making Brazil a leader of the enemy forces was certainly an imaginative touch. Of course it was possible that Brazil had discovered that the village was empty and then had dared to pass through it. Perhaps he had been fleeing from the animals.

Approaching the pen, Magnuson discovered it undamaged, though as Red Circles had said its door stood open and the one-handed hominid was gone. Magnuson had believed Red Circles, but seeing this for himself was still a blow. At least, he noted with relief, there were no signs of violence in or around the pen.

As quickly as he could, he searched the whole village, hut by hut, calling gently. There was no hominid.

The creature might possibly have gone back to the familiar laboratory-pen, near the quarry. As soon as he had checked the last empty hut, Magnuson hurried in that direction, toward the Workers' Village.

From ahead of him, somewhere downstream, there came an odd sound that he could not identify

—as of a metal gong being struck sharply, once. Magnuson paused, listening for a few seconds, but the noise was not repeated. He hurried on.

When the young men of The People ran off in a howling gang with Yellow Monster, Food-Giver watched them out of sight, and then debated with himself what he should do. He had said that he thought the attack on the villages was unwise, but it looked like it was going to be made anyway.

At last, Food-Giver followed the attackers downstream. He was not jealous — at least not consciously so — but he was very curious. Yellow Monster said what he wanted done in a way that made the listener feel it would be wrong to do anything else. Even though Yellow Monster rarely gave food to anyone, still the young men were eager to follow him toward the dangerous villages. There was a great power in Yellow Monster somewhere.

It was necessary to go slow when approaching the villages. Food-Giver found himself a big club to take along, and he was ready at every step to turn around and run for his life. When Yellow Monster and the young hominids ran shouting into the first village, Food-Giver stayed back and waited to see what would happen. Not much of anything seemed to happen, which surprised him; at least there were no sounds of fighting.

Food-Giver was still not convinced. He skirted the empty village suspiciously. The young hominids and Yellow Monster had now got too far ahead for him to see them, but his ears and his nose told him that they were going on downstream.

Remembering another raid of six generations ago, Food-Giver visualized the location of the next village. He made himself go a little faster; he wanted to know whatever was going to happen next, good or bad.

He was drawing near the next village when he heard a call like that of wild hominid children in distress, but in deeper adult voices. It came from ahead and to his right.

"The Dark People," Food-Giver whispered aloud. He took a tight grip on his club. He was alone in enemy territory, and afraid, but he could not ignore that cry. He was a leader because nothing meant more to him than helping his people, and now the Dark People were calling for help.

Food-Giver had a memory, many generations old, of their place of torture, a deep senseless hole dug into stone. He knew where it was, and he moved toward it with slow caution.

On a path ahead, he saw a couple of elderly villagers in kilts hurrying through the woods in frightened silence, coming toward him. They had not seen him, and it would be an easy matter to kill them. But any noise might bring warriors, so Food-Giver hid and waited for the two old people to pass. Then when they were out of sight he went carefully on toward the quarry he remembered but had never seen with his own eyes.

Very slowly, senses alert, he came out of the woods near the lip of the quarry. Here he found much fresh hominid sign, and could recognize the scent of one or two individuals. After considering the sign for a while, he interpreted it to mean that the twenty-

five young men, or most of them anyway, had here
turned north again in the general direction of home.
They were going scattered out through the woods,
and taking with them other hominids who could
only be the Dark People from the pit.

Food-Giver made a sound and gesture of relief.
All this was good, very good. The villagers had been
robbed of their slaves. The People, instead of suffering great loss on this expedition as Food-Giver had
feared, would have their numbers increased. The
Dark People could be given to drink from the Sacred
Pool, and then thought would come into their eyes,
and speech to their tongues, and they would be real
people at last. The tribe had been strengthened.
Yellow Monster and his strange powers had done
very well.

Moving forward to peek down into the quarry-pit,
which was considerably deeper than he remembered
it, Food-Giver saw three gray figures huddled together far below him. He saw that they were not
bound, or confined inside a pen. They were alive,
and free to climb out, but still they stayed in the pit.

"Hey there!" he shouted to them, forgetting
caution for a moment. "Do you want to be Dark
People always?"

But they only huddled together and stared at
him, as if they wanted him to go away.

So. If they refused help, he would not try to force
it on them. He would go home, where he belonged.
But he had left the quarry only a few paces behind
him when he caught a glimpse among the trees of a
thing he did not remember. A strange, big hut, not
such as the villagers usually made but built of the

branchless bodies of many trees placed close together. Curious as always, Food-Giver approached
the structure. The area near it smelled very little of
villagers, but strongly of both monster and hominid.
That seemed to Food-Giver like a friendly
combination, and he was emboldened to go closer.

There was a dark hole, like a cave, let into the
cleverly arranged log-pile. Inside, someone moved,
making timid sounds.

The freshest smell was hominid, so Food-Give
dared to go to the door and look inside. A one-
handed male hominid was there, bedraggled and
frightened-looking. Food-Giver noted the recent
small wounds that marked the other's body, and
stared at the old scar that ended the arm-stump. It
was astonishing how neatly the hand had been
removed, and how its owner had survived such a
loss.

Then Food-Giver remembered to be courteous.
"Are you Dark?" he asked. "Or do you think?"

The eyes of the one-handed hominid were strange
and wild, as if thought were flickering up and down
like firelight behind them. His mouth worked uncertainly. "I . . . I . . . I . . . "

"Maybe you drank once and no more from the
Sacred Pool," said Food-Giver. "That's not enough.
You will come with me now and drink some more."
Food-Giver tried to talk the way Yellow Monster did,
stating positively what should be done. It seemed
that great things could be accomplished by using
such a method. "Also you probably need food and
ordinary water."

Something small squeaked and scuttled in a

corner of the cabin. With an unthinking flash of movement, Food-Giver knocked obstructions aside and struck at the rat with a hunting thrust of his club. The sudden movement and noise made the one-handed one scream as if he were being attacked, and cower away into a corner.

Food-Giver had just made certain of the crippled rat, when he heard running footsteps outside the cabin. He turned sharply, but the breeze brought only a fresh whiff of monster. Food-Giver waited expectantly.

Walking quickly past the rim of the quarry, Magnuson peered down. Sledges and ropes and other tools were scattered carelessly. There had evidently been a hominid raid, the kilted overseers and artisans had fled, the quarry hominids had been taken away. But three of them were still down there in the pit. Perhaps because they knew no other place, perhaps because fear of their masters still held them when their masters were gone. Their up-turned faces, as expressionless as those of cows, followed Magnuson as he walked along the rim. I will not fail you, Magnuson pledged silently, looking down at them. I will yet raise you up into the sun.

There came a sharp clatter and a thump from ahead of him, followed at once by a hominid scream. Inside his laboratory! If the wild ones were in there, and the one-handed man—

Magnuson ran forward. He found the machine pistol ready in his hand.

As Magnuson burst into the cabin he saw the one-handed hominid huddled down in a corner, looking

up at him beseechingly. Before Magnuson could say
or do anything, a big wild one lunged at him out of
the gloom.

The automatic pistol hammered, the repeated
concussion deafening in the enclosed space. One-
Hand screamed once more, and was silent, cowering
away from the noise. The wild one was hurled back
across the room, and torn nearly in half. A table had
already been upset, lab equipment broken, and a
murderous club lay on the floor.

There were no others. Shakily, Magnuson lowered
the pistol. He had come just barely in time, it
seemed, but the new human life was safe.

Something curious struck his eye, and he prodded
with a toe at the nerve-twitching gray hand that had
almost reached him. Beside the hand lay half the
body of a rat. Curious.

Boris, still walking in the direction in which the
priest had pointed, halted when he reached the edge
of the clearing and saw the copter under the trees on
the other side.

"Brenda?"

"Boris?" And her blessed head appeared in one of
the copter ports, to be joined a second later by
Jane's. "Boris, this thing won't fly, the controls are
all smashed. But whoever did it forgot the radio. I
got a message off half an hour ago, when the
villagers all ran away. The colony took a bearing on
us, they're sending an armed copter. Oh, you look so
ridiculous in that little net. But you're alive . . ."
And even before she got out of the copter, Brenda
began to sob.

Boris kissed her, and gobbled half of an emergency ration that Jane found in the copter and brought to him. He kissed both girls, ate the other half of the ration, then crawled into the copter himself and found a spare coverall and put it on.

"Don't want to look ridiculous. Let's start hiking, ladies."

Brenda was still limping a trifle, but ready to go. They had made about three hundred meters east along the shore of Great Lake when the copter from the colony arrived and picked them up.

Seven days later, Boris was walking once more across the common of the Temple Village, through pouring rain. The landing clearing nearby had been enlarged, but was still full of copters. All three of the muddy villages were swarming with Space Force uniforms. The cruiser had arrived at last, and was in orbit above the greenish clouds.

In the middle of the common, Boris passed a villager who stood still, as if perhaps too bewildered to shelter himself from rain. The steady downpour had washed the colored clay from his arms, but Boris knew him. When Boris made a peace gesture, the war chief only looked the more bewildered. After giving Boris a brief sullen stare he turned and walked heavily away, a man whose normal world had been yanked out from under him, never to return.

Some of the Earth's old primitives had believed that a rain such as this fell to mark the death of a great chief. Magnuson was not dead, not the one for whom the heavens groaned and wept today;

Magnuson sat alone in his well-built hut, his face tired but showing an inner contentment.

He looked up at his visitor without much surprise, as if perhaps Boris had been in his thoughts. "Brazil. It wasn't personal enmity that made me help them hunt you. You understand that?"

"You mean Morton forced you?"

Magnuson hesitated. "He would have tried to force me. But I can't say that he did."

"You mean it was for the cause. The great purification of mankind."

Magnuson folded his hands on the rude table before him. "I told you once that none of us matter, much, as individuals."

Boris shook his head slightly. "Anyway, I've already given my statement to the Tribune. Have you heard it or read it?"

"No. I've been ordered to stay in this hut. They'll charge me formally when I've obtained counsel." Magnuson was sitting while Boris stood, but still Boris got the impression that Magnuson was looking down at him. "You know, my hominid is alive and well."

"Your hominid?"

"I think I may claim credit for him. There are Space Force people examining him now. The day before the Space Force came, I succeeded in teaching him a word or two of speech. So you see that the rite of passage was effective."

Boris, sure now that Magnuson did not yet know the truth about the hominids and the Water, stood there feeling weary, and could discover in himself no wish to destroy the smiling assurance before him. It would be short-lived before the Tribune's coming wrath—or else it would perpetuate itself by sliding completely into self-delusion.

Magnuson said: "I was only just in time to save him from a wild one, you know. I wonder what name he'll choose, when he starts to understand about names."

"'Food-Giver' is a good name," said Boris. "Might call him that."

"I don't believe I understand."

"No, I don't believe you do." Boris had just come from viewing Food-Giver's corpse. There had been none of his people nearby when he died, no one to open the skull properly and in time, to drain and preserve the observations of his generous life for future generations.

The rain of the chiefs was falling.

The People: grunting, flea-picking, much abused and cheerful. Nasty, virtuous, and short. They were Boris's people too, now, in a real sense, and he meant to do what he could for them in the future.

But Boris could also remember Brenda being led into this village, to this very hut, helpless in the hands of those who might have killed her in their greed and lust. And he remembered Magnuson cutting the cord that bound her hands, throwing the cord aside, cursing whatever bound human beings, whatever stunted them or made them less than perfect.

"Magnuson, I'll do what I can to help you. You've drunk the Water of Thought several times. What you've done here you may have done under its influence."

"No, we both know that the effect soon passes. My actions here have been sane and responsible. The credit or blame is mine."

"The big charge will be manslaughter, or maybe even murder."

"Why, I don't see any way they can base that. I didn't kill Jones, he was quite willing to enter the ordeal. I didn't kill Kaleta. I've killed no one."

Boris could not stay in the hut any longer, and walked out into the rain. Behind him he could still hear the proud, dedicated voice: "In fact, no one can now deny that I have *created* a new human life from . . . "

Back from a trip to hominid territory, where he had introduced the Tribune's repesentatives as friends, Boris found Brenda waiting for him outside the colony's main gate. She was wearing a rain hood, which she lifted obligingly so he could kiss her. Then she snuggled up against him.

So young. Never been anywhere, really. Offworld once, she had told him, on one quick trip. Such a small-town girl. In the last week he had seen her hunger for children and home-making.

Boris experienced a terrible sinking feeling, akin to what he had heard about drowning. Visions of future changes and responsibilities rose before him. But he was helpless, as if again in the grip of the Water of Thought.

"Listen." He started to walk with Brenda in the rain. "I'm a planeteer. I'm stationed here and there, and I'm moving around all the time. At least that's the kind of work I've always done. I've never been married. I've never wanted to settle down—before. I . . . am I going to have to struggle through this whole speech before you tell me yes or no?"

"You've never said no to me," she said.

THE END

JANET AULISIO ©1980

FRED SABERHAGEN